PUGNAPPED!

COMMANDER UNIVERSE SAVES THE DAY (SORT OF)

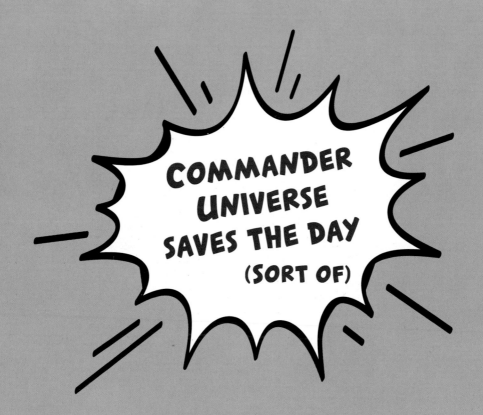

MARTY KELLEY

PUGNAPPED!

STERLING CHILDREN'S BOOKS

New York

FOR THE REAL HEATHER AND HOT JOHN;
TWO OF THE KINDEST, MOST GENEROUS PEOPLE I'VE EVER MET.

AND FOR TIM PUTNAM AND HIS STUDENTS AT CSDA,
WHO HELPED ME IMMEASURABLY ON EARLY VERSIONS OF THIS STORY.

STERLING CHILDREN'S BOOKS
New York

Sterling Children's Books and the distinctive Sterling Children's Books logo
are registered trademarks of Sterling Publishing Co., Inc.

ISBN 978-1-4549-4559-8

Distributed in Canada by Sterling Publishing Co., Inc.
c/o Canadian Manda Group, 664 Annette Street
Toronto, Ontario M6S 2C8, Canada
Distributed in the United Kingdom by GMC Distribution Services
Castle Place, 166 High Street, Lewes, East Sussex BN7 1XU, England
Distributed in Australia by NewSouth Books
University of New South Wales, Sydney, NSW 2052, Australia

For information about custom editions, special sales, and premium
and corporate purchases, please contact Sterling Special Sales at
800-805-5489 or specialsales@sterlingpublishing.com.

Manufactured in Malaysia

Lot #:
2 4 6 8 10 9 7 5 3 1

07/21

sterlingpublishing.com

Cover and interior illustrations by Marty Kelley
Cover and interior design by Shannon Nicole Plunkett

AN IMPORTANT MESSAGE FROM

COMMANDER UNIVERSE

Attention, citizens of Earth. My name is Commander Universe. I am a superhero with dozens of amazing superpowers. I developed my powers after a villainous mastermind sprayed me with millions of gallons of toxic waste.

I wrote down my epic adventures for the benefit of the human race. I even added some museum-quality Action-Vision artwork now that I have Super Drawing Powers. It's so realistic, you'll feel like part of the action. I'm sure the art will help make this thrilling story even more spectacular.

Please enjoy this book in complete safety, knowing that whenever danger threatens, Commander Universe will be there to save the day.

AWAY TO JUSTICE!

I'LL START WITH . . .

Chapter 1

MY ARCH-ENEMY

"Hey, nerd-burger!" yelled a voice behind me. "What are you doing out here in your pajamas?"

Rudy and I spun around to see my arch-enemy, The Parasite, standing at the door of Comic World. He glared at me with his beady, evil eyes and burst into cackling laughter. "Mwaaa Ha Ha Ha Haaaaaaaaaa!"

"Oh, man," Rudy groaned. "I am not in the mood for Chaz Pharsight right now."

"What do you want, Parasite?" I snapped.

"I want to know why you're running around the neighborhood in your little jammies, doofus."

"These are not pajamas," I explained in a deep, heroic voice. "This is a sleek, aerodynamic superhero outfit."

"And what is that all over your face? Did you draw on yourself with a marker?"

"That is my mask, Parasite."

"And what did you do to your hair?" The Parasite sneered. "It looks like you glued a buttered gerbil on your head."

"I told you that hairdo was a mistake, dude," Rudy whispered.

I shooshed Rudy and ran my hand over my perfectly sculpted superhero hair. "I used my mother's super-hold hair gel. It's called style, Parasite."

"Stop calling me Parasite, weirdo. My name is Chaz. What is wrong with you?"

"See the cape?" I asked, flapping my cape. "See the mask and the amazing superhero outfit? See the super-heroic hair? I am Commander Universe. And this is my sidekick, Rudy."

"I'm not your sidekick, dude," Rudy sighed.

"More like Commander Gooniverse. You have a pillowcase pinned to your shoulders." The Parasite laughed again. "You get weirder every day, Stevie."

I gasped.

How could The Parasite possibly have recognized me? I spent hours in my secret laboratory yesterday creating a superhero outfit that would hide my true identity of mild-mannered Stevie Blunt. My disguise was foolproof and my hair was absolutely perfect.

"Who is this Stevie person?" I asked, looking around. "I am Commander Universe. I don't know anyone named Stevie. Although he certainly sounds like a smart, handsome, and very cool person."

"He's not. He's a weirdo dork-o-rama who runs around town in his pajamas with marker all over his face," The Parasite sneered. He reached for the door. "Why don't you fly back to planet Goofball? I'm here to buy the first issue of *Captain Fantastic* that Mr. Falcetti just got."

"You're too late, Parasite," I said, giving him **SUPERHERO LOOK #8: DRAMATICALLY ARCHED EYEBROW**. "The first issue of *Captain Fantastic* is mine."

"What?" cried The Parasite. "You bought it?"

"I still can't believe you're going to waste $75 on a stupid comic book," Rudy said.

"A stupid comic book?" I gasped. "This is no ordinary comic book, young Rudy. This is the very first issue of *Captain Fantastic*. There were only 1,000 copies ever printed. It contains his personal training journal, where he explains how he developed his incredible skills after he was involved in a terrible toxic waste spill. The training journal is top secret, and everyone who reads it must swear an Unbreakable Oath of Secrecy. The only way to find out what's in it is to get that comic book. And now I've got it."

"No, you don't. You didn't have the $75 to pay for it," Rudy said. "Mr. Falcetti said that he'd hold it for you until Monday."

"That's right. And once I get my hands on that top-secret training journal, I will learn how to control these amazing powers I'm developing."

Yesterday, I was involved in a tragic accident. A twisted supervillain covered me with millions of gallons of toxic waste. Now I'm developing incredible superpowers, just like Captain Fantastic. I will be the world's newest, greatest superhero . . . Commander Universe.

THE SECRET ORIGIN OF
COMMANDER UNIVERSE

YESTERDAY I WAS SPRAYED WITH MILLIONS OF GALLONS OF GLOWING, RADIOACTIVE TOXIC WASTE.

OOPS. I GOT SOME PUDDING ON YOUR SHIRT, STEVIE.

AHHRRRGG!

← Super Cool Transformation

UMMM . . . WHAT ARE YOU DOING, MIJO?

Millions of Gallons of Toxic Waste

WHAT HAVE YOU DONE TO ME YOU VILLAINOUS SUPER-CRIMINAL?

↑ Villainous Super-Criminal

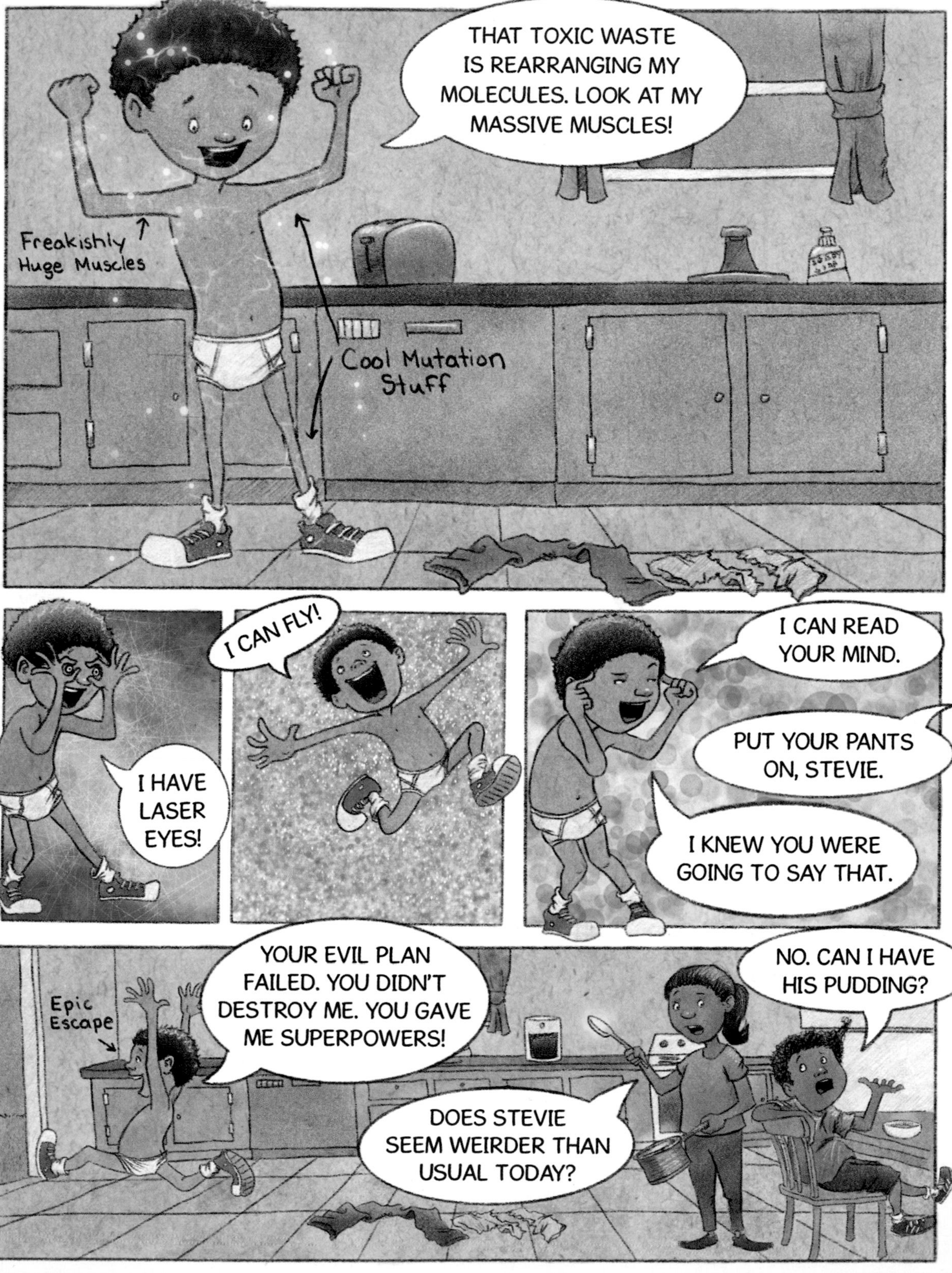
THAT TOXIC WASTE IS REARRANGING MY MOLECULES. LOOK AT MY MASSIVE MUSCLES!
Freakishly Huge Muscles
Cool Mutation Stuff
I HAVE LASER EYES!
I CAN FLY!
I CAN READ YOUR MIND.
PUT YOUR PANTS ON, STEVIE.
I KNEW YOU WERE GOING TO SAY THAT.
Epic Escape
YOUR EVIL PLAN FAILED. YOU DIDN'T DESTROY ME. YOU GAVE ME SUPERPOWERS!
DOES STEVIE SEEM WEIRDER THAN USUAL TODAY?
NO. CAN I HAVE HIS PUDDING?

"Where are you going to get $75, Stevie?" The Parasite laughed. "You probably don't even have 75 cents. My father gives me money to buy whatever I want. I'm going in to buy that comic book right now. It's the only one I'm missing from my *Captain Fantastic* collection. After I get it, I'll have every issue ever printed. And you'll still just be hanging around out here in your pajamas like the super goober that you are."

I jumped in front of him. "Oh, no you don't, Parasite. I won't let you use that training journal for evil."

"Get out of my way, Commander Pajamaverse." He pushed past me and reached for the door of Comic World just as Mr. Falcetti flipped the sign in the window to "CLOSED." Mr. Falcetti stepped out the door, locking it behind him.

"Wait! Mr. Falcetti!" The Parasite cried, yanking a wad of cash from his pocket. "I have money. I want to buy *Captain Fantastic!*"

"Sorry, kid," Mr. Falcetti answered. "Closing early for the weekend. It's my wedding anniversary. I'm taking Mrs. Falcetti out for an afternoon movie and the Early Bird Special at that fancy new French restaurant, *La Maison des Oeufs Verts au Jambon.*

Coolest Hair Ever!

Super Power Drink

Top-Secret Documents

And anyway, I said I'd hold that comic till Monday for Stevie."

I gasped again. How could he possibly have recognized my true identity?

"Looks like your evil plans have failed again, Parasite," I said, standing in **SUPERHERO POSE #142: HANDS ON HIPS**.

The Parasite laughed another evil laugh. "Mwaaa HA HA HA HAAAAAA! You'll never come up with $75 by Monday, Commander Weenieverse. But I'll tell you what. I'll let you use your Weenie-Vision to watch *me* read the first issue of *Captain Fantastic*."

He jumped on his jet-powered rocket cycle and blasted off down the street toward his evil lair.

"I'm going home," Rudy said. "My mom made more pistachio pudding. I'd invite you to come over, but she's still kind of mad that you called her a villainous super-criminal and yelled about her pudding rearranging your molecules."

I was halfway back to my headquarters when a blood-curdling scream echoed through the neighborhood. . . .

Unusual Helmet Design for Evil Villain

Jet-Powered Rocket Cycle

Training Wheels?

Chapter 2

MY OTHER ARCH-ENEMY

NOOOOOOOOOOOOOOO!

EGADS! THAT SOUNDS LIKE MISS BOYLE!

Superhero Pose #71:
Listening Carefully

I SPRANG INTO ACTION. MY HAIR WAS PERFECT.

Glittery
Heroic
Awesomeness

AWAY TO JUSTICE!*

*MY EPIC BATTLE CRY.

I ROCKETED TO MISS BOYLE'S HEADQUARTERS USING MY SUPER-SPEED BLAST-O-MATIC TURBO THRUST POWER

NANOSECONDS LATER, I SKIDDED TO A STOP NEXT TO AN UNFAMILIAR VEHICLE IN MISS BOYLE'S DRIVEWAY.

Miss Boyle is the prettiest lady in our whole town. She has long brown hair and rainbow-painted toenails that look like a birthday party. She always wears flip-flops so people can see her party toes.

I have my suspicions that Miss Boyle may actually have superpowers of her own. She zips around the neighborhood on a candy-apple-red hovercraft, occasionally disintegrating evildoers with her sonic death blaster.

"Oh, Stevie," she laughed, wiping the tears from her cheeks. "Is that marker all over your face? And what did you do to your hair? It looks like you have a greased-up weasel on your head."

"It's a mask!" I cried. "And my hair is spectacular! And I'm not Stevie. I'm Commander Universe. I was involved in a tragic toxic waste spill and I've developed amazing superpowers. I'm here to save the day."

Miss Boyle smiled. "I need a hero like you, Stevie."

"Commander Universe," I corrected. "I don't know anybody named Stevie. Although he sounds like a wonderful, charming, and very good-looking person with amazing hair. What is your emergency, citizen?"

"Oh," Miss Boyle sighed. "It's awful—"

Before she could finish, a snarling beast the size of a school bus thundered around the corner of Miss Boyle's house, its steely jaws dripping ropy strands of sizzling acid. Razor-sharp fangs jutted from its horrible black gums. Its deadly claws raked the ground, spraying sparks in its wake. The earth shook as the creature barreled toward us. It howled and launched itself into the air. I threw myself in front of the monster.

It was time to be a hero. . . .

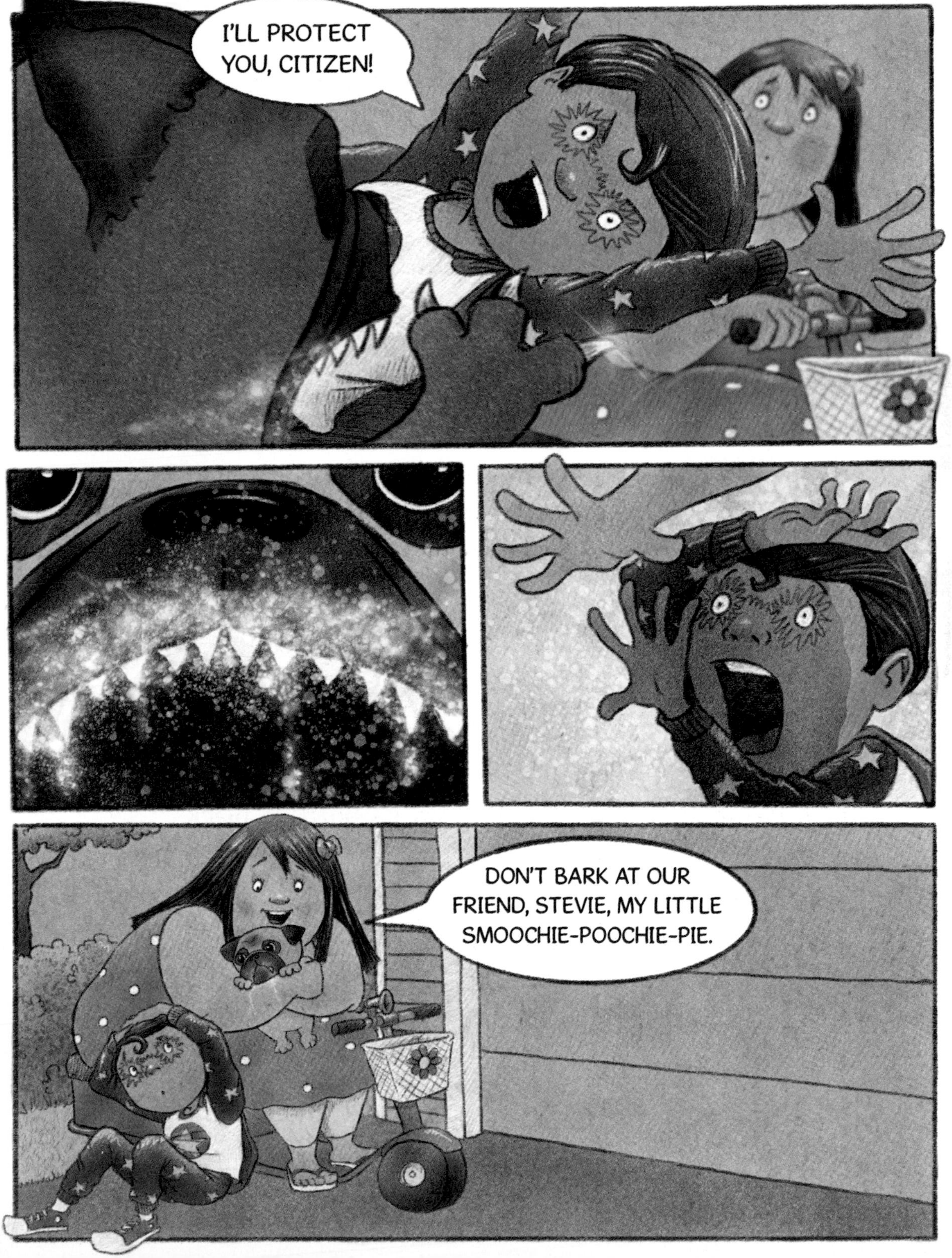
I'LL PROTECT YOU, CITIZEN!
DON'T BARK AT OUR FRIEND, STEVIE, MY LITTLE SMOOCHIE-POOCHIE-PIE.

She patted the beast's belly. "Don't you be a naughty puppy, Cupcake. You be nice to Stevie."

Miss Boyle sighed. "It's my precious little Cupcake's birthday today and I'm driving to Boston to pick up a cake for the party tonight."

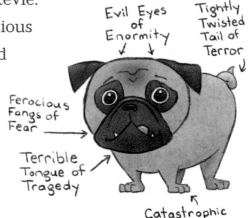

Evil Eyes of Enormity

Tightly Twisted Tail of Terror

Ferocious Fangs of Fear

Terrible Tongue of Tragedy

Catastrophic Claws of Concern

"You're driving all the way to Boston for a birthday cake?" I asked. "For your dog? Boston is a two-hour drive from here."

"Oh, yes," Miss Boyle answered, scratching the evil monster's head. "I took my little Cupcake to the Pug Olympics in Boston last year, and we discovered this amazing little bakery in the North End. They had an incredible triple-almond torte, made with imported almonds and organic, free-range, gluten-free flour and cream from pasture-raised cows. My little pookie-snookums loved it so much, didn't you? Didn't you, you wittle cake-nibbling sweetie-poops? So, of course I'm driving there to get one for my little snuggie-wuggums's birthday party. Nothing is too good for Mama's wittle baby-waby." Miss Boyle slumped in her hovercraft. "At least, I *was* driving there today."

"Is your vehicle disabled?" I asked, inspecting it for signs of damage. "Perhaps I can fix the problem with my Thermal Weld-O-Vision."

"No," Miss Boyle sighed. "Cupcake's personal activity specialist just called with awful news: they have fleas in their recreation center. I can't send my precious little lovie lumpkins someplace that has fleas. And I can't take her to Boston with me because she gets carsick. We had to take a train the last time we went, and she got so upset on the ride home that I had to schedule extra sessions with her puppy therapist and she had to take anti-anxiety medication. I don't know what I'm going to do. If I don't get that cake, my poor little scruffy-wuffy's birthday party will be ruined. I'll never find anyone else who can watch her on such short notice. My precious little Cupcake needs so much special attention."

This was my first chance to help a citizen in distress.

"I'll help you, citizen. Give me the coordinates of the bakery. I'll fly there and return with the cake."

"Oh, Stevie," Miss Boyle sighed. "I wish you could."

"You're right," I said, nodding. "The cake will probably get ruined when I blast through the sound barrier. Maybe I could use my Mind-Meld Brain Control Power to hypnotize Cupcake so she won't get carsick."

"No," Miss Boyle said. "We tried hypnosis once when we went to a mommy/puppy spa weekend. My little Cupcake didn't do well with that. At all."

I strained to think of any way I could help Miss Boyle. This was my big chance to use my amazing new powers.

21

"I don't dare call one of the other canine recreation coordinators in town," Miss Boyle said. "The last time I did that, I got charged $250 for the day and she didn't even bother to read the directions I left. She served my little sweetheart a tenderloin steak that was cooked medium. Cupcake always has her tenderloin cooked medium rare. My poor little lamby-kins was very upset for days. I had to take her to extra therapy sessions."

"You paid a dog-sitter $250?" I gasped.

"Not a dog-sitter," Miss Boyle corrected. "A canine recreation coordinator. They're highly trained expert play facilitators."

I puffed out my mighty chest. "I'll watch Cupcake for you, Miss Boyle."

Miss Boyle looked at me with eyes like twin bowls of chocolate ice cream.

"What?" she asked. "You, Stevie?"

"Me. Commander Universe." I said, standing in **SUPERHERO POSE #27: CALM AND CONFIDENT**.

Miss Boyle shook her head slowly. "I don't know, Stevie. . . ."

"I don't know Stevie, either," I said. "I keep telling you, I'm Commander Universe."

Miss Boyle smiled. "Well, Commander Universe, Cupcake is a very delicate little puppy."

Cupcake growled and bared her razor-sharp fangs.

"She needs to be looked after very carefully," Miss Boyle continued. "Can I trust you to look after my precious little snuggle-bug?"

I raised my eyebrow and smiled. "Of course you can, citizen. And naturally, I won't charge you $250. Superheroes never work for money. But $75 would help me save the planet from The Parasite and his evil plans."

Miss Boyle laughed. "I'll tell you what, Commander Universe. If you'll watch Cupcake this afternoon so I can get her birthday cake, I'll pay you $100."

"$100?" I cried.

"One. Hundred. Dollars." Miss Boyle said. "This is an emergency. I really need someone reliable and heroic to watch Cupcake for me this afternoon. It would cost me more than twice that much to hire someone I don't even know. And she won't get fleas from you. I hope."

Miss Boyle winked at me.

I winked back at her and adjusted my cape.

It was time to be a hero.

Chapter 3

MY SIDEKICK, X

After a quick call to my headquarters to arrange details with The Chief, Miss Boyle handed me a bulging three-ring binder crammed with top-secret instructions for guarding Cupcake.

There were 17 pages describing how Cupcake needed to be brushed and groomed, 56 pages about what she could and could not eat, a schedule of her favorite TV shows, 6 pages of telephone numbers for her medical specialists, 3 pages of directions (with photos) for cleaning the wrinkles in Cupcake's face so she doesn't get "stink-face," a list of approved music and activities, and about 150 other pages of stuff.

There was also Mr. Woobles.

Mr. Woobles is a squeaky, plastic clown that looks like it has been chewed, swallowed, barfed back up again, and then

Disgusting Drool of Despair

Tooth Marks of Terror

MORE Tooth Marks of Terror

run over with a lawnmower, smashed with a hammer, and chewed up some more.

"Mr. Woobles is Cupcake's favorite toy ever," Miss Boyle explained, squeaking the awful thing a few times in Cupcake's stink-face. "You love Mr. Woobles, don't you? Don't you? Don't you?"

Cupcake howled with joy and chewed Mr. Woobles loudly and sloppily while Miss Boyle explained the difference between Cupcake's four toothbrushes. She was demonstrating how to hold the liver-flavored, organic dental floss when a man strolled out of Miss Boyle's backyard. He wore a bright yellow T-shirt with "Hot John" printed across it in huge red letters. He had a pair of Death-Ray Goggles on. His arms were covered in strange, evil symbols. The scruffy little beard thingy on his face made it clear that this man was an evil supervillain. . . .

Death-Ray Goggles

Vaguely Unpleasant Supervillain Facial Hair

Hot John's TV Systems
867-5309

Strange, Evil Symbols

Diabolical Device

Suspiciously Large Boots

HE RAISED HIS HAND AND REVEALED A DIABOLICAL DEVICE, THE LIKES OF WHICH I HAD NEVER SEEN BEFORE.

Terrifying Device

HALT, VILLAIN. PUT DOWN THAT MYSTERIOUS DEVICE. DON'T MAKE ME DESTROY YOU.

Superhero Pose #9-c: Halt Villain

WHOA THERE, TOUGH GUY. WHAT ARE YOU DOING OUT HERE IN YOUR PAJAMAS? AND WHAT IS UP WITH THAT HAIR?

John's Systems 7-5309

I USED MY SUPER-FREEZE BLAST BREATH ON HIM.

Ice Crystals

IT HAD NO EFFECT.

HERE YOU GO. IT'S ALL SET.

THANK YOU, HOT JOHN.

Miss Boyle's eyes sparkled like a really big disco ball covered in a million bike reflectors and fireworks. She lifted Cupcake and strapped the strange device around the beast's neck.

"There," she announced. "That's your first birthday surprise, my precious little treasure. The nice man installed PuppyVision for you!"

Cupcake barked and yipped.

"PuppyVision?" I asked, eyeing the device. "What sort of evil scheme is that?"

The man laughed a deep, villainous laugh. "It's not a scheme. And it's not evil. It's a total entertainment system for the dog who has everything—only available from Hot John's TV Systems. PuppyVision comes complete with surround sound, a high-definition 84-inch plasma screen, and a customized, programmable, hands-free remote control unit that I invented. Plus," he added, smiling at Miss Boyle, "I'll throw in free 24/7 customer service. Just for you."

He pointed to the device that Miss Boyle had strapped to Cupcake's neck.

"The micro-processor in this box reads the dog's brain waves and changes the channel based on what the dog wants to see. PuppyVision offers over 450 channels. All designed for dogs."

"It reads Cupcake's mind?" I gasped.

"Well . . . sort of," Hot John explained. "It measures changes in the brain's magnetic energy field and switches to a channel that reflects the wearer's current mood. You can fine-tune it with this small knob on the side of the box."

This was obviously some nefarious mind-control technology, complete with a Dial of Misery.

Hot John would have to be added to my list of dangerous supervillains. Before I could question him further, Miss Boyle gasped.

"I've got to go! It's a long drive to Boston, and if I don't start right now I'll never make it back in time for Cupcake's birthday party dinner! Cupcake gets very upset if her dinner is late."

Hot John drove away in his mobile command unit, and Miss Boyle spent another five minutes slobbering good-byes all over Cupcake.

Finally, Cupcake and I stood at the end of the driveway and watched Miss Boyle leave.

As soon as her van turned the corner, Cupcake glared up at me with evil, buggy eyes and exploded into a frenzy of yapping and howling. I searched through the binder to find out how to calm her down, but found nothing. I tried using

Super
Calm
Stuff

my **CALM-O-VISION** on her, but it only seemed to anger her more.

I was going to need help, and there was only one person I could trust with a job this important: my faithful sidekick, Rudy.

I secured Cupcake inside her puppy condo and raced off to Rudy's secret headquarters. Seconds later, I arrived to find him sitting on his front steps, eating a gallon-sized tub of the same toxic waste that I had been sprayed with yesterday.

"Come on!" I cried. "I've been asked to guard Cupcake for the day. The forces of evil are everywhere! I need assistance. Go change into your superhero outfit!"

"What?" Rudy asked, licking his spoon.

Using my Hyper-Drive Explaining Power, I was able to persuade Rudy to help me.

"You're getting $100 to babysit Miss Boyle's evil little dog?" Rudy asked.

"Of course, superheroes never work for money . . ."
I began.

"I'll help you for $25," Rudy said.

"But . . . I . . ."

"Deal!" Rudy cried, running into his house.

He burst through the door moments later wearing a
T-shirt with a picture of a giant eyeball scrawled across it
in blue magic marker. He had a cone of aluminum foil
wrapped around his head.

He was also wearing
a pair of goggles made
out of pipe cleaners
with waxed paper
where the lenses
should have been.

"Uh . . ." I pointed to
the goggles, "What's with
those?"

Rudy looked
over the top of
them. "I hate to
admit it, because
this seems totally ridiculous,
but I guess you were right.

Cone of
Brain
Safety ™

Wonder
Goggles →

Tape Measure
of Truth

Duct Tape
of Justice

11mm
Wrench of
Retribution

Ever since you agreed to give me $25, I realized that my mom's pudding must have given me superpowers, too. I have X-Ray Vision. When I was in my house just now, I heard someone call my name from the other room. I knew it was my mom, so I can obviously see through walls! My superhero name will be X! I made these Wonder Goggles to block out some of the more disgusting sights."

"Can you see through those at all?" I asked.

"Not really," Rudy admitted. "But I need them. Otherwise I'll be looking through everybody's clothes all the time. Nasty."

Rudy had his father's toolbelt wrapped around his waist. He dug through a pocket and yanked out a small silver device. "I've also got my Tape Measure of Truth!" He dug through another pocket. "And my 11-Millimeter Wrench of Retribution and The Duct Tape of Justice."

Rudy tapped the cone of aluminum foil wrapped around his head. "Plus I've got my high-impact titanium Cone of Brain Safety™ to protect my brain and to keep my hair from getting messed up during spectacular fights. Now let's go keep Cupcake safe from the forces of evil!"

We raced down the street at nearly the speed of light. . . .

Cool Sonic Boom Stuff

STAY OFF MY LAWN, HIPPIES!

WE SKIDDED TO A STOP NEXT TO CUPCAKE'S PUPPY PENTHOUSE. WE NEEDED TO PLAN A SNEAK ATTACK.

SHHH. THE EVIL BEAST MUST BE WAITING TO TEAR US LIMB FROM LIMB. TAKE A LOOK, X.

ME?

← Super Sneaky Mode

YOU HAVE THE X-RAY VISION.

WHAT IS THE SITUATION, TRUSTY SIDEKICK?

Sidekick Butt-Crack

WE HAVE A BIG PROBLEM, DUDE.

CUPCAKE IS GONE! ON THE PLUS SIDE, THESE TREATS ARE DELICIOUS.

Chapter 4

THE DOGGONE DOG IS GONE, DOGGONE IT

I quickly scanned the interior of Cupcake's condo with my Scan-O-Vision. Bright sunlight streamed in through the three skylights. The hot tub steamed and bubbled in the corner next to a puppy-sized refrigerator stocked with Cupcake's favorite treats. The far wall was completely covered by the gigantic new PuppyVision system that Hot John had installed.

Everything was right where it should be—the cappuccino machine, the heated waterbed, the massage table.

Everything except Cupcake.

"Cupcake is gone!" I cried.

"Um . . . yeah," Rudy said, looking over his Wonder Goggles. "I just said that. Maybe you should work on your Super Paying Attention Power."

Rudy picked up the indestructible steel cable that had been attached to Cupcake's collar. "It's been cut!" he gasped.

I grabbed the cord from Rudy's hand. "Yes," I said, inspecting it with my Microscope-O-Vision. "It has been cut."

"I just said that, too, dude. Have you considered changing your name to The Annoying, Repetitious Parrot Boy?"

I sprang into **SUPERHERO POSE #9: THINKING HARD**.

"If Cupcake isn't here," I said, pacing across the yard. "Then that means—"

"That means you're a dead man," Rudy interrupted. "Miss Boyle hasn't even been gone for 15 minutes, and you've already let Cupcake run away. Miss Boyle loves that dog more than anything in the world. She's going to kill you. Can I have your bike when you're dead?"

"No," I said.

"But my bike has a wobbly front tire from the time I tried to jump over the—"

I shushed Rudy with a blast from my Super-Freeze Breath.

"If we don't find Cupcake, Miss Boyle is going to be heartbroken," I said. "She trusted me because I'm a superhero . . . and I let her down. She's always so cool, racing us on her hovercraft and giving us cookies. And now I've lost her dog. I am a disgrace to superheroes everywhere. I can't believe it."

I crumpled to the ground in a heap.

"Plus," Rudy said, pulling me back up to my feet, "if you don't find Cupcake and get the money, Chaz is going to buy that comic."

"No," I said, gazing off into the middle distance. "If The Parasite gets that journal, he will do unspeakable evil with it. We can't let that happen."

I paused for dramatic effect and let the sunlight glimmer over my lustrous Super Hair.

"Cupcake has been kidnapped. This is just like issue #976 of *Captain Fantastic*, when the President's prized poodle, Puddles, is kidnapped by the evil dog groomer, Groomerella McKlipz, who wants to use Puddles to win the World Dog Show, collect the $10,000,000 prize, and then use the prize money to buy a time machine so she can go back in time and win all the dog shows in history and become the richest, most powerful dog groomer in the entire world. It all makes perfect sense."

"Nope," Rudy said. "That makes no sense at all."

"This is no time to make sense," I said. "This is a time for action! Away to Justice!"

Rudy grabbed my cape. "Away to Justice? Is that your

battle cry? That's pretty weak. I'm going to come up with a way better battle cry than that."

"We don't have time for this! We need to rescue Cupcake! Away to Justice!" I launched myself into the clear, summer sky to search for clues from the air, but Rudy grabbed my cape again and yanked me back to earth.

"We have to rescue Cupcake! Stop grabbing my cape," I cried.

"I don't get it, dude." Rudy said. "Why would someone kidnap Cupcake? She's the most vicious, annoying dog in the entire world."

"Miss Boyle loves Cupcake, right?"

"I think it's fair to say that she loves that dog even more than I love my mom's pudding," Rudy agreed.

"And if some evil supervillain managed to kidnap Cupcake, that supervillain could force Miss Boyle to pay billions of dollars in ransom to get Cupcake back, right?"

"Wrong," Rudy said, shaking his head. "Miss Boyle doesn't have billions of dollars."

"She must," I said. "How else do you think she could afford to buy Cupcake a cappuccino machine?"

"Hmmmm. Good point," Rudy admitted.

"So some evil villain has obviously kidnapped Cupcake in order to get billions of dollars in ransom money from Miss Boyle. And we're going to stop him."

"Stop who?" Rudy asked.

"The supervillain," I answered. "My newest, evilest, archest arch-enemy."

"Who is . . . ?" Rudy asked.

"I'm not sure," I admitted.

"So you don't even know who your arch-enemy is?" Rudy asked. "Dude, come on. You really need to think this stuff through."

"We will find this villain," I continued, puffing out my huge, manly chest and placing my hands on my hips. "And we will bring him to justice. Or else—"

"Or else Miss Boyle will kill you and I'll get your bike!"

"Let's go!" I cried, yanking Rudy toward the street with my Incredible Super Strength. "We've got to find Cupcake. The fate of the entire universe depends on it."

We nearly collided with Abi Chan, our neighbor who lives down the street. She was dressed in a black turtleneck, black sneakers, striped tights, and a raspberry-colored beret. She wore a mask cut out of crinkled construction paper.

"Behold!" Abi cried, holding up her hands and waving around a pair of oven mitts. "It is I: Abi, the Amazing Hero of Super-Awesome Incredibleness!"

"Abi!" I cried. "Why are you dressed like that? You look like an explosion at a clown factory."

"A clown factory?" Rudy asked. "What the heck is a clown factory?"

Abi pointed to the black turtleneck, mask, and sneakers. "I'm dressed in black so I can disappear into the shadows."

I pointed to the bright pink beret. "And that?"

Abi shrugged. "Every superhero should have a little pop of color for style. Maybe you should consider a stylish hat of some sort to cover up whatever is going on with your hair. It looks like you strapped a wet beaver to your head."

"This is official superhero hair," I said. "And why are you dressed up like a bank-robbing mime with a cherry on top?"

"I saw you guys being superheroes and I want to be a superhero, too. I'm Abi, the Incredible and Amazing Super Girl of Incredible Powerfulness and Deceptive Cuteness."

"That's not the name you just told us a few seconds ago," I said. "Come on, Rudy. We've got to go."

Abi grabbed my cape and stopped me. "My superpowers are so amazing that I need a new name every few seconds."

"Dude," whispered Rudy, "that IS amazing."

"It's not amazing," I cried. "It's ridiculous! You can't just change your superhero name every few seconds."

"Yes, I can," Abi said. "I can do anything because I'm . . . dun dah doo, dundundun duuuunhn . . . Awesome Abi McSuperDuper!"

"Whoa!" Rudy gasped, staring at Abi. "She has a theme song!"

Definitely NOT invisible.

"And I can turn invisible. Watch!" Abi flicked her hands in front of her face. "Whashaaaa! I'm invisible."

"WHOA!" cried Rudy. "She even has sound effects! Wait! Where is she?! I can't see her!"

"Your Wonder Goggles are covering your eyes," I sighed. "Now can we please go? We've got an important mission."

Rudy lifted his goggles. "Oh. Yeah. There she is."

"You can only see me because you have X-Ray Vision," Abi said. "I'm invisible."

"I can see you, Abi," I said. "And I don't have X-Ray Vision. We have an emergency situation here. We've got to go! Away to Justice!"

Abi grabbed my cape again.

"You can see me because I want you to see me. Only people I want to see me can see me. And I want you to see me because we're being superheroes together."

"No, we're not," I told her. "We're on an important mission."

Abi crossed her arms. "I heard you guys saying that you lost Cupcake. And if you don't let me be a superhero with you, I'll tell Miss Boyle that you lost her doggy and Miss Boyle will kill you and Rudy will get your bike."

"Totally true, dude," Rudy agreed.

We were wasting precious time arguing with Abi. My new Think-O-Matic Incredi-Brain instantly developed a brilliant plan to deal with her.

"Fine," I said. "You can be a Super Guy with us, Adequate Abi of Whateverness."

"My new name is Captain Super-Colossal-Avenger-Death-Grip-Lightning-Bolt of Wonder."

"Dude!" Rudy cried. "That is seriously the coolest superhero name ever. I'm totally jealous. She has a theme song, sound effects, and those super-cool gloves!"

"All right, Abi," I sighed. "I'm giving you a top-secret mission. Go search the neighborhood for clues." I pointed down the road. "Go. Report back to us when you find something."

Abi saluted and ran off down the street.

I smiled cunningly. "Abi might think she can turn invisible, but I made her disappear. Now let's go find Cupcake and bring the kidnapper to justice."

Chapter 5

EVIL, MUTANT SQUIRRELS AND A NOISY CLUE

I ran up and down the street, calling Cupcake with my Ultra-High-Frequency Dog Calling Power.

"Will you stop making that awful squeaking noise? You sound like a deranged squirrel." Rudy wandered along behind me, looking for clues in Cupcake's binder. "Did you know that Cupcake gets terrible gas if she eats anything with dairy in it? If we ever find her, we should give her some milk and see if she develops super fart powers. I totally need that superpower. I'd be all like, 'Hey. You. Bad Guy. Freeze or I'll blast you with my terrifying Fart of Justice.' And then, BOOM!"

Rudy pointed to the binder. "And did you know that Cupcake loves chasing squirrels? It says here that if Cupcake sees a squirrel, we're supposed to call her therapist immediately, because otherwise—"

I froze. My Hyper Hearing detected a strange sound nearby. . . .

I HELD UP A HAND AND SHOOSHED RUDY WITH MY POWER SHOOSH.

SHHHHH!!! DID YOU HEAR THAT?

Power Shoosh →

IT'S COMING FROM DOWN THERE!

Hyper Hearing

YOU MEAN UP THERE?

YES. UP IN THE TREE. WHAT IS IT? USE YOUR X-RAY VISION!

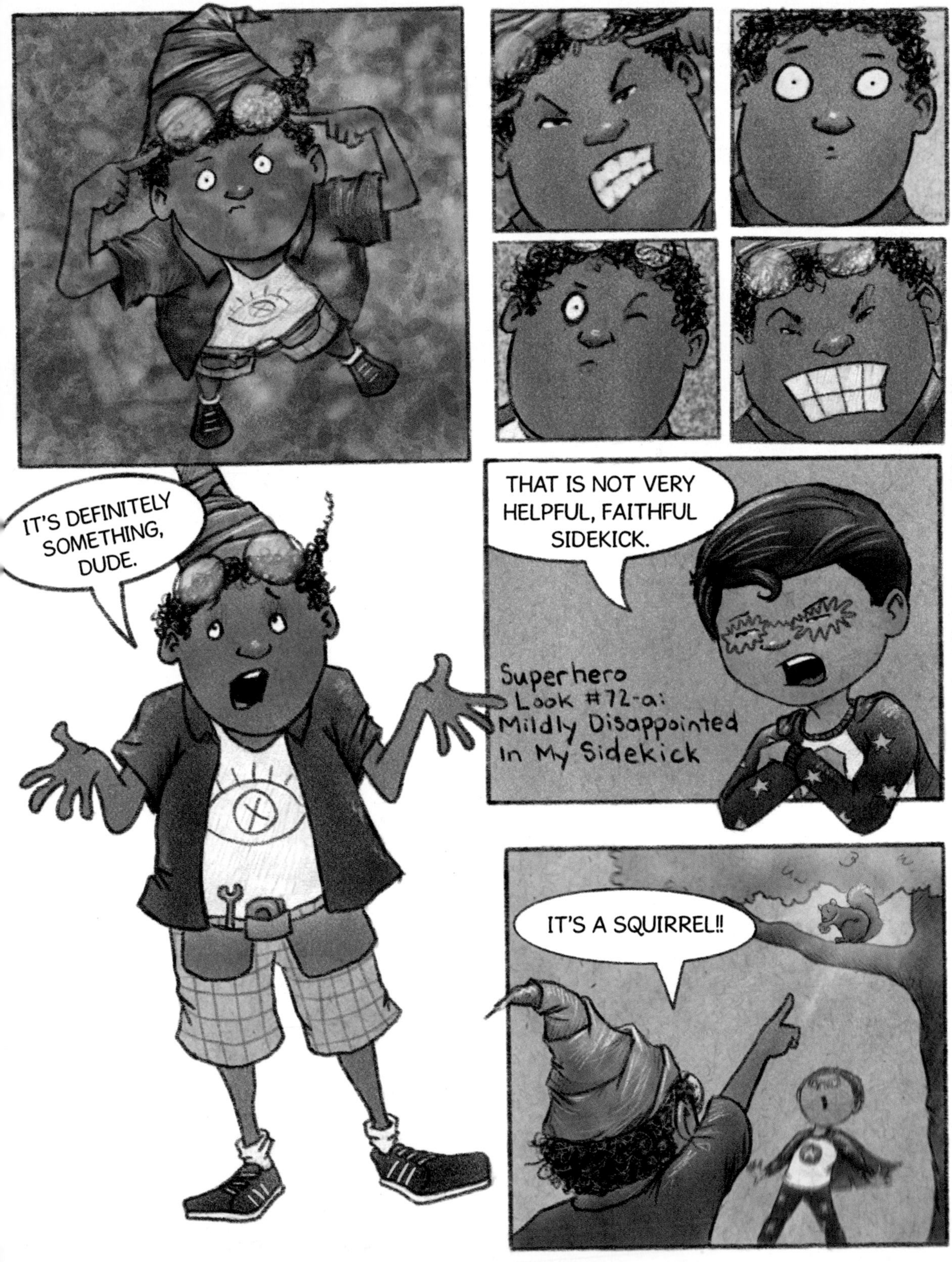
IT'S DEFINITELY SOMETHING, DUDE.
THAT IS NOT VERY HELPFUL, FAITHFUL SIDEKICK.
Superhero Look #72-a: Mildly Disappointed In My Sidekick
IT'S A SQUIRREL!!

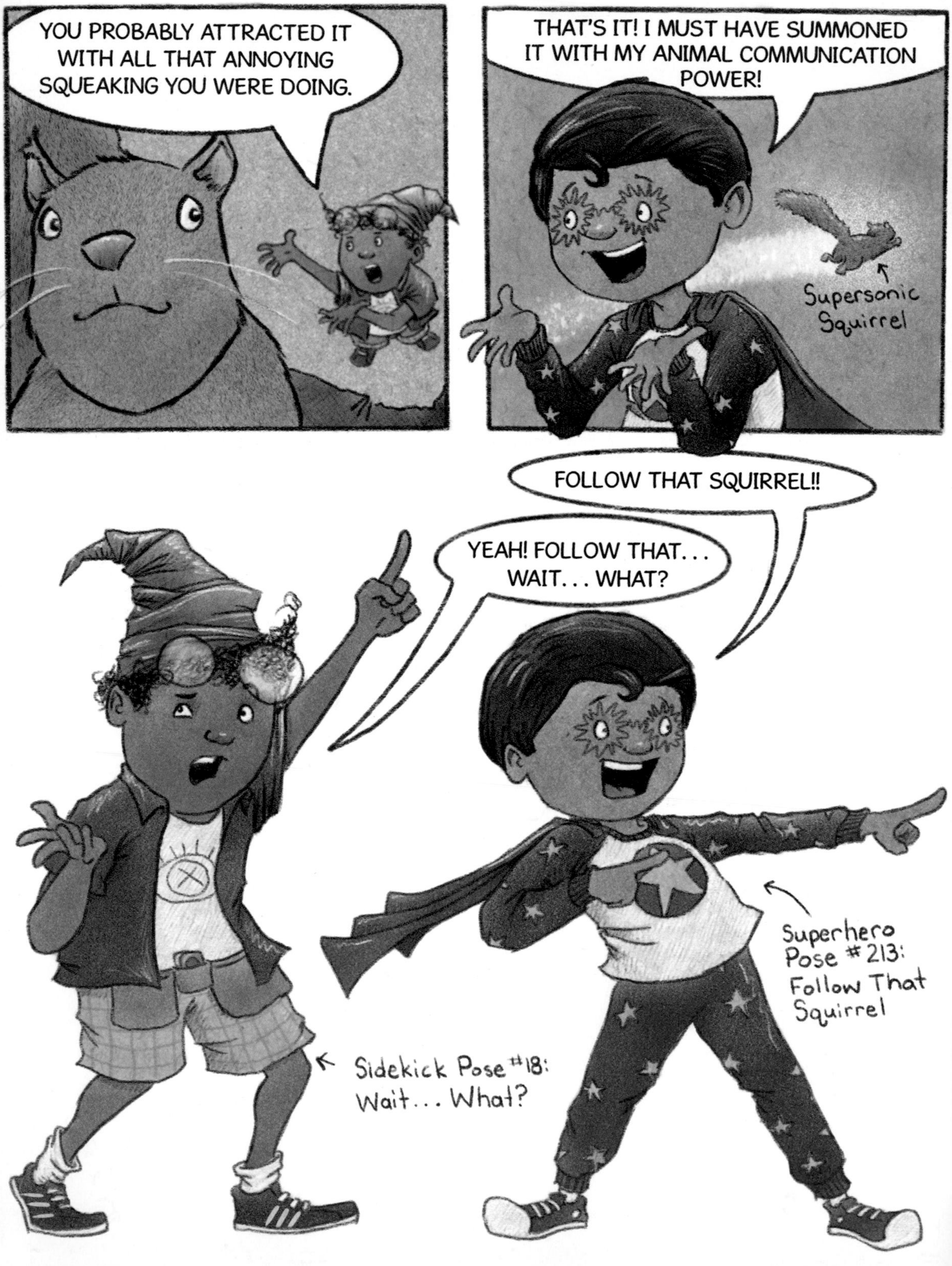
YOU PROBABLY ATTRACTED IT WITH ALL THAT ANNOYING SQUEAKING YOU WERE DOING.
THAT'S IT! I MUST HAVE SUMMONED IT WITH MY ANIMAL COMMUNICATION POWER!
Supersonic Squirrel
FOLLOW THAT SQUIRREL!!
YEAH! FOLLOW THAT... WAIT... WHAT?
Superhero Pose #213: Follow That Squirrel
Sidekick Pose #18: Wait... What?

"It's just like issue #1671 of *The Zookeeper* when The Zookeeper adds two stray weasels to his animal army but they're really weasel commandos who were brainwashed by The Zookeeper's arch-enemy, Fleabag. The Zookeeper loved them so much that it snapped them out of the mind-control brainwashing, freeing them from Fleabag's evil clutches. Then they became part of The Zookeeper's Family Fun Petting Zoo of Happy Fuzziness. It all makes perfect sense."

Rudy rubbed his forehead. "Dude, do you realize that your ideas of things that make perfect sense are actually making less and less sense?"

"It does all make perfect sense. Cupcake is missing, right? Cupcake chases squirrels, right? So obviously the kidnapper must have used mutant brainwashed squirrels to chew through Cupcake's leash and lead her away. All we have to do is grab that squirrel and I'll use my Super Animal Communication Power to find out what it knows."

"Too bad you spent so long talking, Commander Yaks-A-Lot," Rudy said, pointing down the street. "The squirrel is getting away."

The squirrel must have been a genetically modified Super Squirrel because that thing was really, really fast.

"Away to Justice!" I cried, launching myself into the air.

"That's still a really terrible battle cry," Rudy said. He threw his fist in the air. "Easy Peasy Lemon Squeezy!"

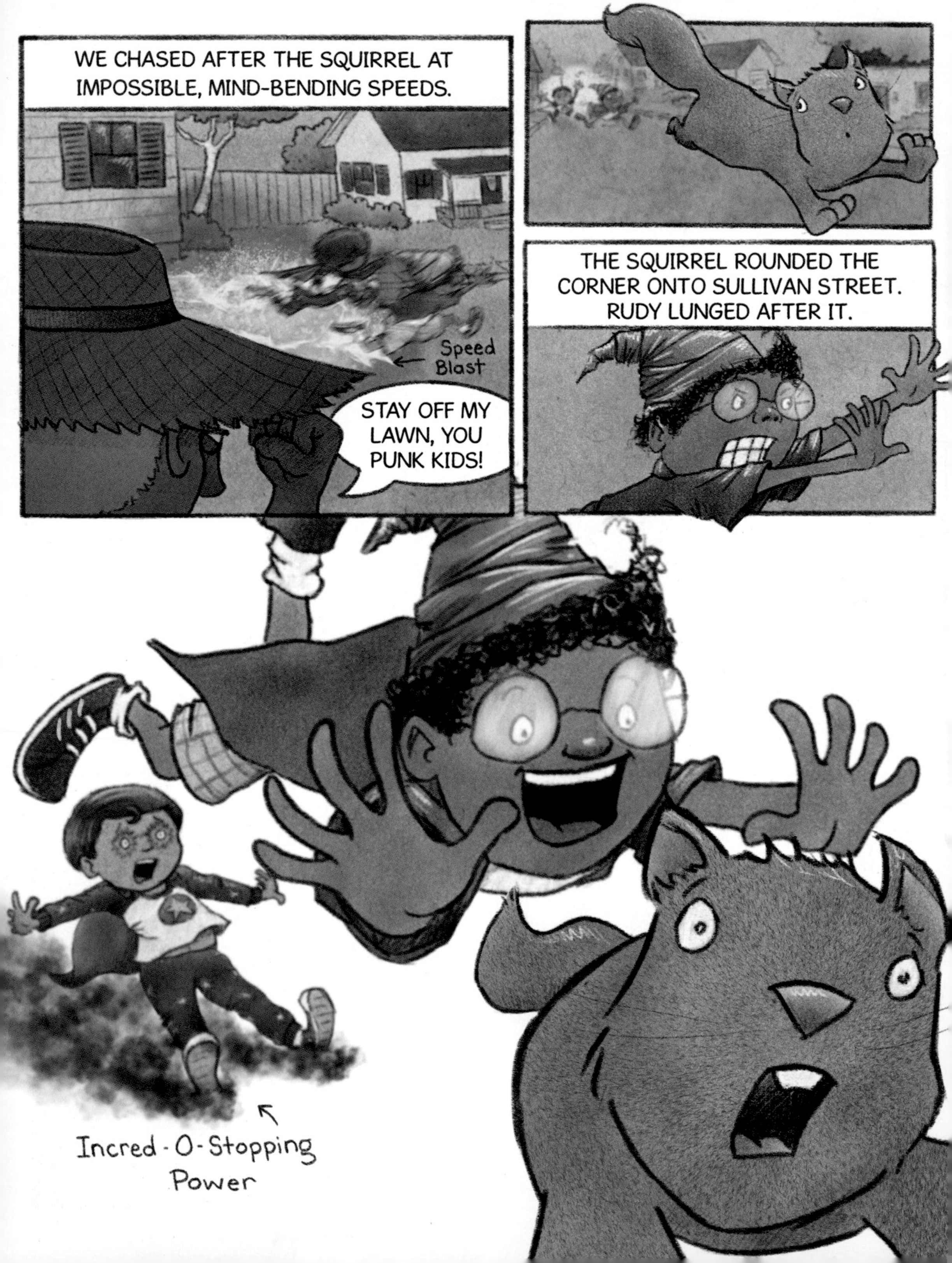
WE CHASED AFTER THE SQUIRREL AT IMPOSSIBLE, MIND-BENDING SPEEDS.
Speed Blast
STAY OFF MY LAWN, YOU PUNK KIDS!
THE SQUIRREL ROUNDED THE CORNER ONTO SULLIVAN STREET. RUDY LUNGED AFTER IT.
Incred-O-Stopping Power

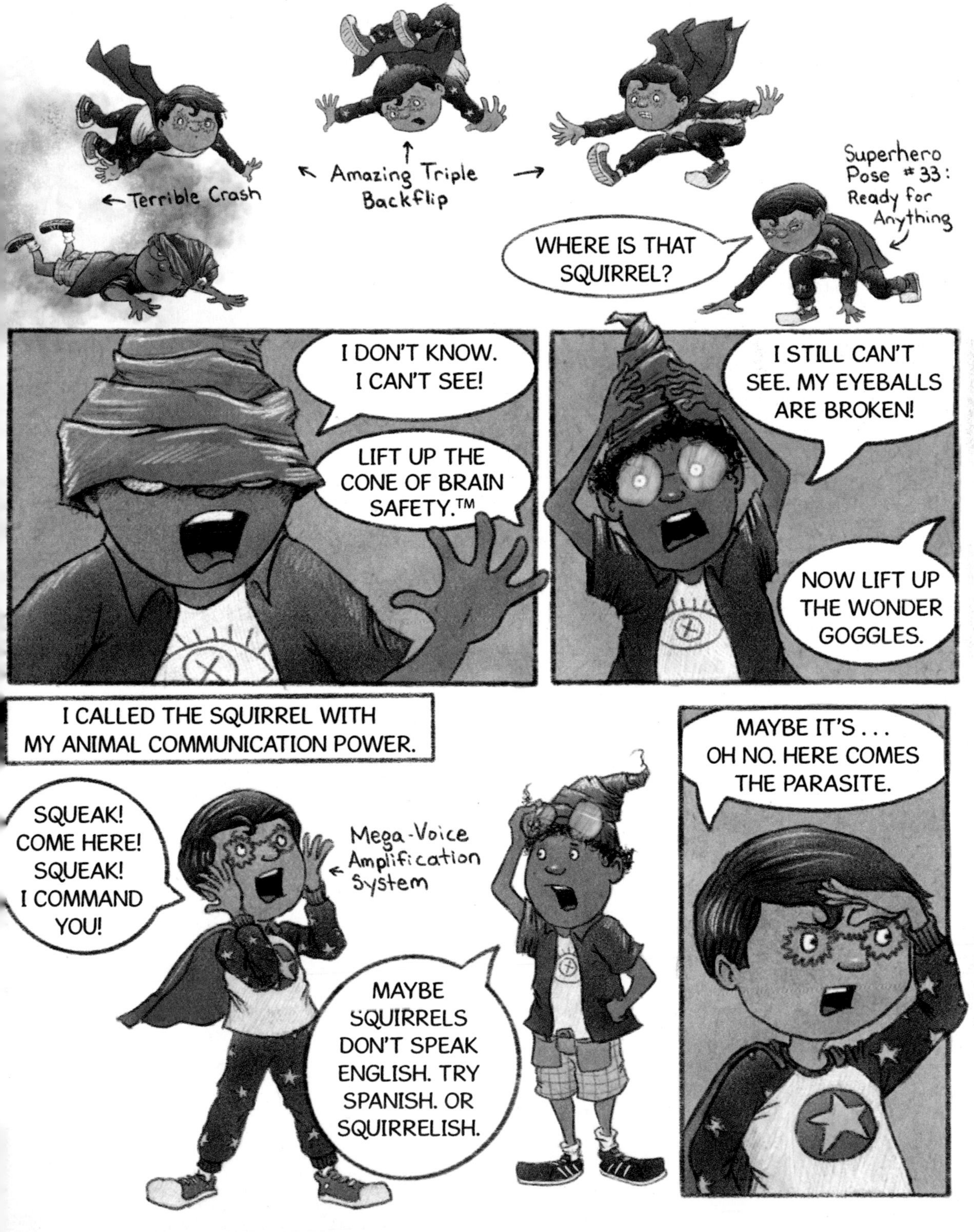

Terrible Crash
Amazing Triple Backflip
Superhero Pose #33: Ready for Anything
WHERE IS THAT SQUIRREL?
I DON'T KNOW. I CAN'T SEE!
LIFT UP THE CONE OF BRAIN SAFETY.™
I STILL CAN'T SEE. MY EYEBALLS ARE BROKEN!
NOW LIFT UP THE WONDER GOGGLES.
I CALLED THE SQUIRREL WITH MY ANIMAL COMMUNICATION POWER.
SQUEAK! COME HERE! SQUEAK! I COMMAND YOU!
Mega-Voice Amplification System
MAYBE SQUIRRELS DON'T SPEAK ENGLISH. TRY SPANISH. OR SQUIRRELISH.
MAYBE IT'S . . . OH NO. HERE COMES THE PARASITE.

"Are you still running around in your jammies, Stevie?" The Parasite sneered.

He was carrying a paper grocery bag with a torn corner. A dribble of dry dog food sprinkled onto the pavement.

"Your lunch is spilling," I said, pointing at the mess on the sidewalk.

The Parasite clamped his hand over the hole. "It's not my lunch, Commander Pajama-Pants."

"You don't have a dog," I said, using my Super Observation Power. "So why would you buy dog food?"

The Parasite flushed bright red. "I'm not the one who was dumb enough to lose Miss Boyle's dog, Commander Fart Sniffer," he spluttered. "Looks like you won't be buying that comic on Monday because Miss Boyle is never going to pay you now."

"Wait a minute," Rudy said. "How did you know that Cupcake was gone?"

The Parasite flushed red again. He must be developing some sort of chameleon powers so he can change colors.

"Because . . . because . . . uhhhh . . . I heard you two yelling about it all the way down the street," he stammered.

He spun around and stormed off, sneering about how he was going to read the *Captain Fantastic* comic book at my funeral after Miss Boyle killed me for losing her dog.

"Come on, Rudy," I said. "We don't have time to deal with The Parasite now. We've got to rescue Cupcake!"

Rudy cupped his hand to his ear. "My X-Ray Hearing has detected something."

"X-Ray Hearing?" I said. "There's no such thing as X-Ray Hearing. You can't—"

"SHHHHH!" Rudy hissed at me.

Rudy held his finger to his lips and pointed to The Mystery Neighbor's house. From a back window came the sound of a dog barking.

"It's Cupcake!" I cried.

Chapter 6

AN ALMOST AMAZING RESCUE

Nobody has ever seen The Mystery Neighbors. Ever. Cars go into the garage. Cars come out of the garage. Lights turn on. Lights turn off. But nobody has ever actually seen The Mystery Neighbors.

They remain . . . A Mystery.

"Why would The Mystery Neighbors kidnap Cupcake?" Rudy asked.

"For the ransom money," I explained. "This is just like issue #212 of *Marvelous Man*, when Marvelous Man's sidekick, Bobo, gets kidnapped by hideous creatures from deep beneath the Earth's crust. They tell Marvelous Man that they will throw Bobo into a pool of molten lava if he doesn't give them all the gold in the world. Then Marvelous Man rescues Bobo at the last minute by smashing through the side of their volcano hideout and flying him to safety. It all makes perfect sense."

"Wait, wait, wait." Rudy said, waving his hands. "Marvelous Man has a sidekick named Bobo? That's the worst sidekick name ever."

"That's not the point!" I cried. "The point is that we have found the evil kidnappers. Now we can rescue Cupcake! We have to hurry. Miss Boyle will be back in a few hours."

"No. But, seriously—Bobo?" Rudy asked.

I glared at him with my **SUPER GLARE**. "We need to rescue Cupcake."

"How?" Rudy asked.

I flexed my mighty biceps. "With loads of amazing flips, kicks, and explosions. And sound effects and loud music and awesome slow-motion fight scenes."

"Maybe we should just go to the front door and ring the doorbell and ask them to give Cupcake back," Rudy suggested.

"What?!?" I cried. "You think we can just stroll up to the high-security front door of our arch-enemy's evil lair and ring the doorbell and ask them to return Cupcake?"

"What if we said 'please'?" Rudy asked.

"No," I said. "Even if it would work—and it wouldn't—it isn't The Superhero Way. This is just like issue #823 of *The Flying Fist of Fury*, when The Flying Fist gets locked out of his Fortress of Fistitude by his arch-enemy, The Hangnail. The Hangnail snuck into the Fortress while The Flying Fist was out getting a manicure. Then The Hangnail piled up all The Flying Fist's furniture against the door so The Flying Fist couldn't get back in. So The Flying Fist flew into the door headfirst with his Flying Fury powers and smashed through the door and took The Hangnail to jail. It all makes perfect sense."

"Wait, what? The superhero was out getting a manicure?" Rudy asked. "What kind of superhero gets manicures?"

"Well," I explained, "The Flying Fist's alter-ego is Phalanges Digit, the world-famous hand model. So he was getting a manicure."

Rudy shook his head. "So, are you saying that we should go get manicures?"

"No," I sighed, pointing to the impenetrable wall surrounding the Mystery Neighbor's compound. "We don't have time for manicures. We need to hurry. I'm saying that we need to smash through that gate."

"And how are we supposed to do that?"

"I can use my **SUPER STRENGTH** to pick you up and use you as a battering ram to smash through the gate. You'll be safe because you're wearing the Cone of Brain Safety.™ Then we can rescue Cupcake and get her back to her condo before Miss Boyle gets home. Then Miss Boyle will be happy and I can collect the money from her and buy the top-secret journal and become the greatest superhero in the history of the world. Come on."

I tried to grab Rudy, but he stepped back.

"No way. You're not going to—"

Rudy was interrupted by more barking from the other side of the fence.

"Come on, faithful Rudy!" I cried, leaping into action. . . .

Battering Rudy

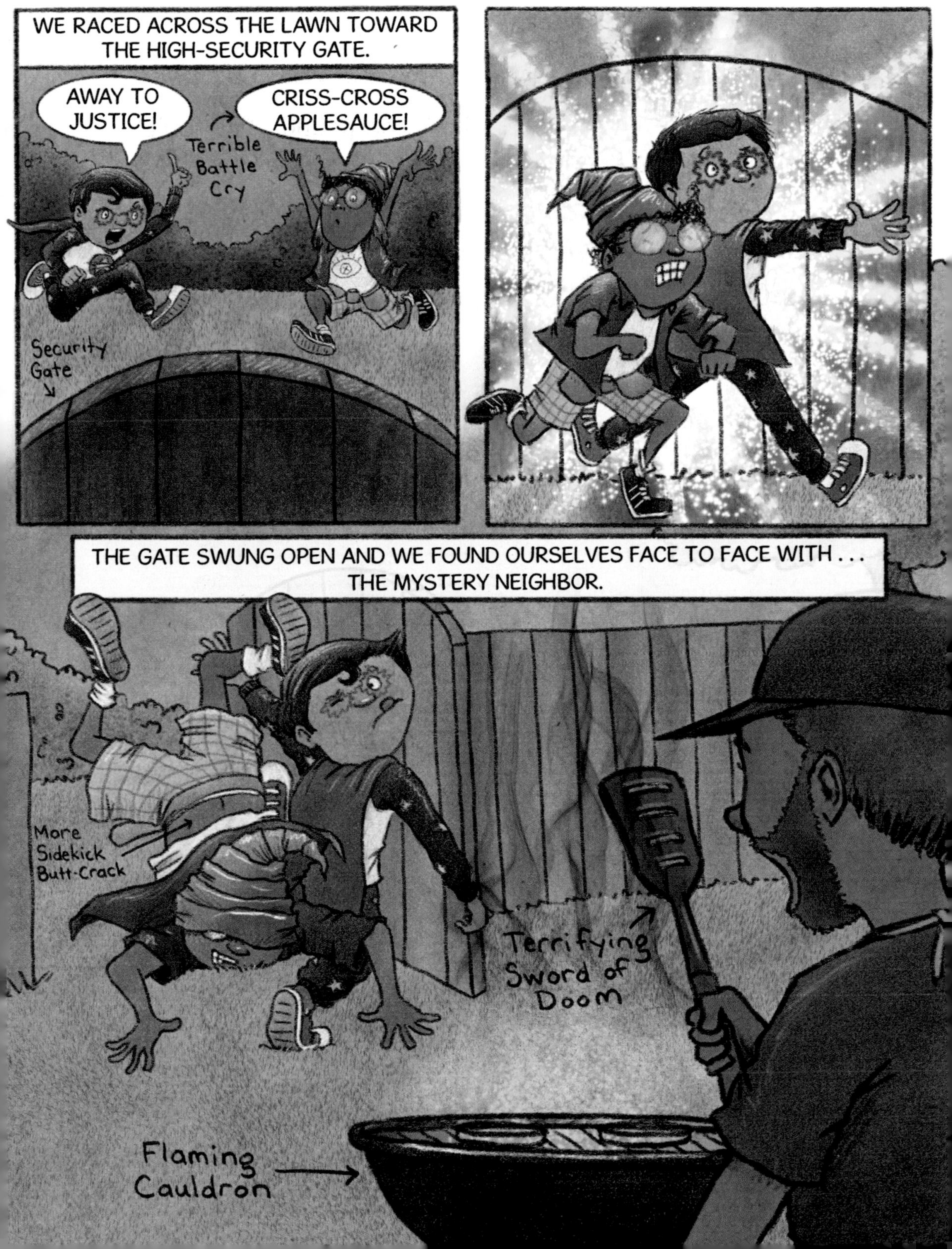
WE RACED ACROSS THE LAWN TOWARD THE HIGH-SECURITY GATE.
AWAY TO JUSTICE!
CRISS-CROSS APPLESAUCE!
Terrible Battle Cry
Security Gate
THE GATE SWUNG OPEN AND WE FOUND OURSELVES FACE TO FACE WITH . . . THE MYSTERY NEIGHBOR.
More Sidekick Butt-Crack
Terrifying Sword of Doom
Flaming Cauldron

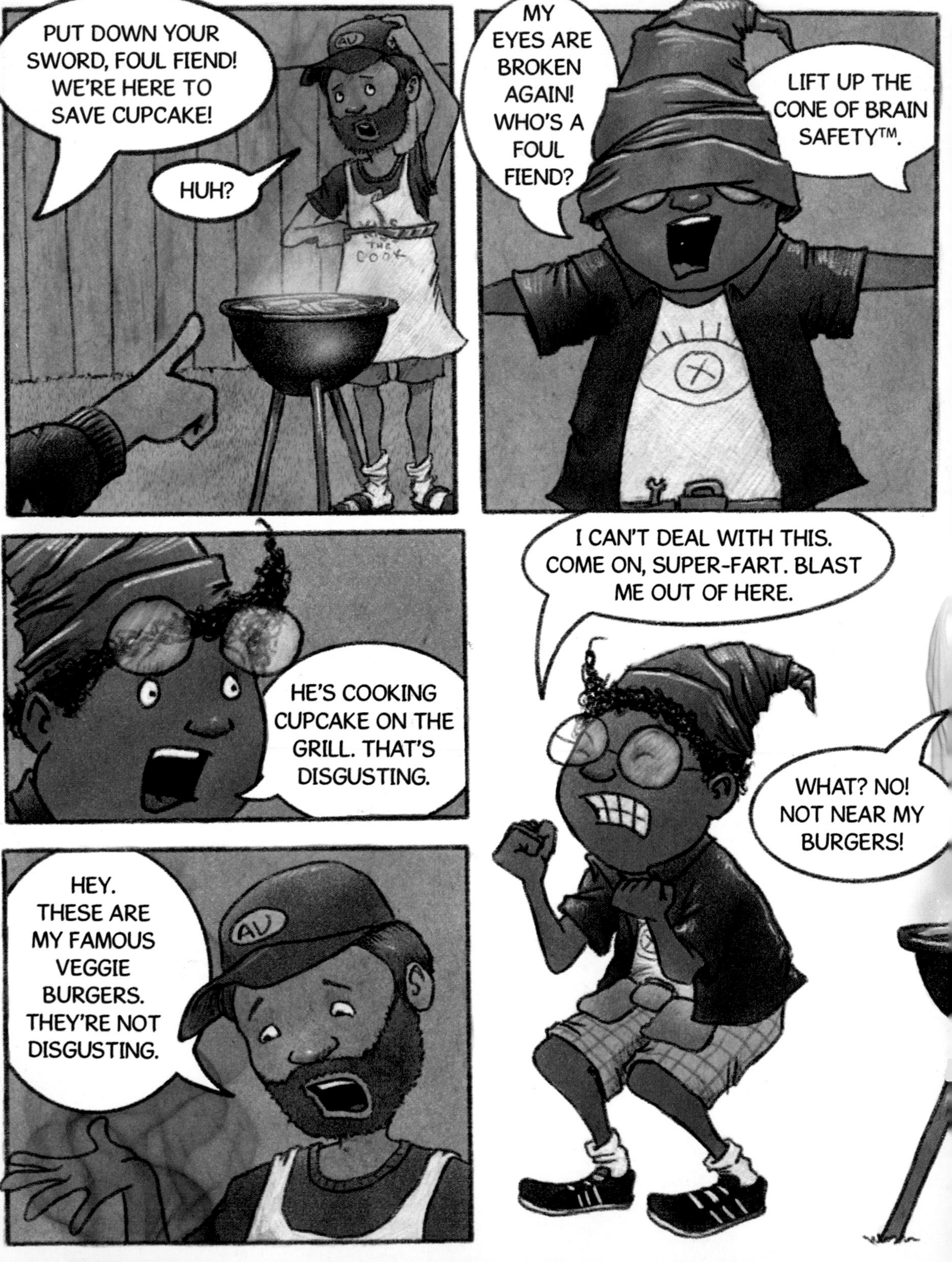
PUT DOWN YOUR SWORD, FOUL FIEND! WE'RE HERE TO SAVE CUPCAKE!
HUH?
MY EYES ARE BROKEN AGAIN! WHO'S A FOUL FIEND?
LIFT UP THE CONE OF BRAIN SAFETY™.
HE'S COOKING CUPCAKE ON THE GRILL. THAT'S DISGUSTING.
HEY. THESE ARE MY FAMOUS VEGGIE BURGERS. THEY'RE NOT DISGUSTING.
I CAN'T DEAL WITH THIS. COME ON, SUPER-FART. BLAST ME OUT OF HERE.
WHAT? NO! NOT NEAR MY BURGERS!

IT'S NOT WORKING!!

RUDY'S SUPER-FART FAILED TO ACTIVATE. HE DESERTED ME IN THE ENEMY'S LAIR.

AHHHHHH!!!

Much Worse Battle Cry

Superhero Look # 72-b: Quite Disappointed In My Sidekick

IT WAS UP TO ME TO FACE THE MYSTERY NEIGHBOR AND BRING HIM TO JUSTICE.

ALL RIGHT, SUPERVILLIAN, YOU CAN'T SCARE COMMANDER UNIVERSE THAT EASILY. IF YOU WON'T TELL ME WHERE CUPCAKE IS, PREPARE TO HAVE YOUR MIND SCANNED.

Superhero Pose #5: Mind Scan Time!

KISS THE COOK

"What the heck are you two doing?" the man wailed. "And why are you in my backyard in your pajamas? And is that an oiled-up wombat sleeping on your head?"

"We're here to rescue Cupcake!"

A tiny lady wearing a lot of makeup stepped through a sliding glass door onto the porch. "Tim! What in the world is happening out here? Are those burgers almost done? Princess is hungry and . . . and . . . and why is there a child with a damp guinea pig on his head in our backyard?"

"It's my Super Hair! I'm Commander Universe, and I'm here to rescue Cupcake!" I announced.

Tim shook his head. "What?"

The woman nodded her head. "Oooohhhhh, Cupcake. I know Miss Boyle and Cupcake. We both belong to the same puppy play-group. They are soooooo sweet. Why in the world would you think Cupcake was here?"

"We heard her barking from the street."

Something small and furry scrabbled out the door behind the lady.

"Cupcake!" I cried.

"Oh, young man," the lady said, turning and picking up the dog, "This is Princess, my prize-winning show poodle. I could never let another doggy come into Princess's yard. This is her private, personal space, and she really doesn't like to share with other puppies. That's why I take her to puppy play-group. So she can learn to get along with other little puppies; even though she's better than them. Isn't that right, my little Princess?" The lady buried her face in Princess's fur and made horrible kissy noises.

Somewhat Cool Doggy Hairdo →

Slightly Less Cool Ankle Hairdo ↙

Super Cool Butt Hairdo

"So, Cupcake isn't here?" I asked.

Before the woman could answer me, Hot John stepped out through the sliding door. "All finished in here, ma'am," he said, holding up an electronic collar identical to the one he had given Miss Boyle. "PuppyVision is ready for Princess."

Hot John's smile faded when he saw me. "Still running around town in your jammies, huh, kid?"

"He was just leaving," Tim said, pointing to the gate.

"Oh, yes, I'm leaving," I announced, adjusting my cape and fixing my hair. "But remember that Commander Universe is here to keep the world safe from bionic mutant dog-napping squirrels."

I strode to the gate with my cape flowing majestically behind me. Rudy's face appeared over the fence. "AH HA!" he cried. "Don't worry, Commander Universe! X has come to save you!"

Rudy launched himself over the fence and flew gracefully through the air for about a half a second before crashing face-first in Princess's food dish.

Chapter 7

THE VILLAIN MAKES A BIG MISTAKE

The Mystery Neighbors were not pleased with Rudy's rescue attempt.

As we marched back out through the gate, my Super Incred-O-Hearing picked up something about crazy kids and too much TV.

"Where's Cupcake?" Rudy asked, picking a wet glob of dog food from his nostril.

"Cupcake wasn't there," I growled. We stood on the sidewalk to have a top-secret, high-level Superhero Meeting. "That evil squirrel wasn't leading us to Cupcake. It was obviously a devious ploy to lead us *away* from Cupcake. Time is running out. We have to find Cupcake before Miss Boyle gets back from Boston. Whoever is controlling those mutant squirrels is obviously even more of an evil genius than I had counted on. He must be using some sort of powerful brainwave amplification device to control the squirrels' minds."

I paced the sidewalk.

"We must search the neighborhood for a suspicious piece of equipment. Something that could be used to transmit powerful mind-control rays to all the squirrels in the area. It could be anywhere."

"How are we supposed to find something like that?" Rudy asked. "We don't even know what we're looking for. And it's not like an evil villain with a huge mind-control device is going to be driving down the street with it, showing it off to the whole world."

At that moment, The Mystery Neighbor's garage door rumbled open, revealing Hot John's mobile command unit. It started up with a growl and backed down the driveway.

Hot John pulled up next to us and waved us over.

"I forgot to give Miss Boyle the bill for the PuppyVision," Hot John said, holding out an envelope. "Do you two superheroes think you can deliver this to her house safely?"

I arched my eyebrow and looked at him with **SUPERHERO LOOK #8-C: SLIGHTLY LESS DRAMATICALLY ARCHED EYEBROW**.

"We're superheroes, not messengers," Rudy said, stepping out briefly from behind the safety of my bullet-proof super cape.

I smiled at Hot John. "Of course we can handle that assignment, citizen. Superheroes are here to help everyone. Even people like you who may, in fact, be supervillains in disguise."

I took the envelope from Hot John, giving him **SUPERHERO LOOK #28: I'M ON TO YOU**. →

"Is something wrong with your face?" Hot John asked. "Looks like you've got gas or something."

"Maybe I do," I answered mysteriously. "Maybe I do. . . ."

Rudy jumped away from behind me.

Hot John crinkled his nose. "Make sure she gets that bill, please."

We watched as he drove slowly away.

"Why are we delivering messages?" Rudy asked. "We're The Super Guys, not The Delivery Guys. We don't have time to deliver messages! We've got a kidnapped dog to find. No dog, no money. No money, no comic. No comic, no training journal. Remember?"

I held up a hand and used my Brain Blast-o-Matic to silence Rudy with my mind.

"Get your sweaty hand off my mouth," Rudy yelped, swatting my hand away.

"We've found our villain," I said, holding up the envelope. "This isn't a bill. It's obviously a ransom note."

"What are you talking about?" Rudy asked. "He just told us that it's a bill."

"Our newest arch-enemy must have a brainwave amplification device, right? Something that he's using to control the minds of innocent squirrels, right?"

"Right," Rudy agreed.

I pointed down the street to Hot John's van as it rounded the corner. "Look."

Rudy's jaw dropped as he saw the satellite dish mounted to the top of Hot John's van.

"We've found our dog-napping villain," I said.

Chapter 8

WE FIND THE VILLAIN, BUT LOSE THE VILLAIN, BUT FIND ANOTHER VILLAIN. ALMOST.

WE CHASED HOT JOHN'S MOBILE COMMAND UNIT DOWN THE STREET.

Suspicious Satellite Dish →

← Hyper-Mega Launch

← Cool Flying Stuff

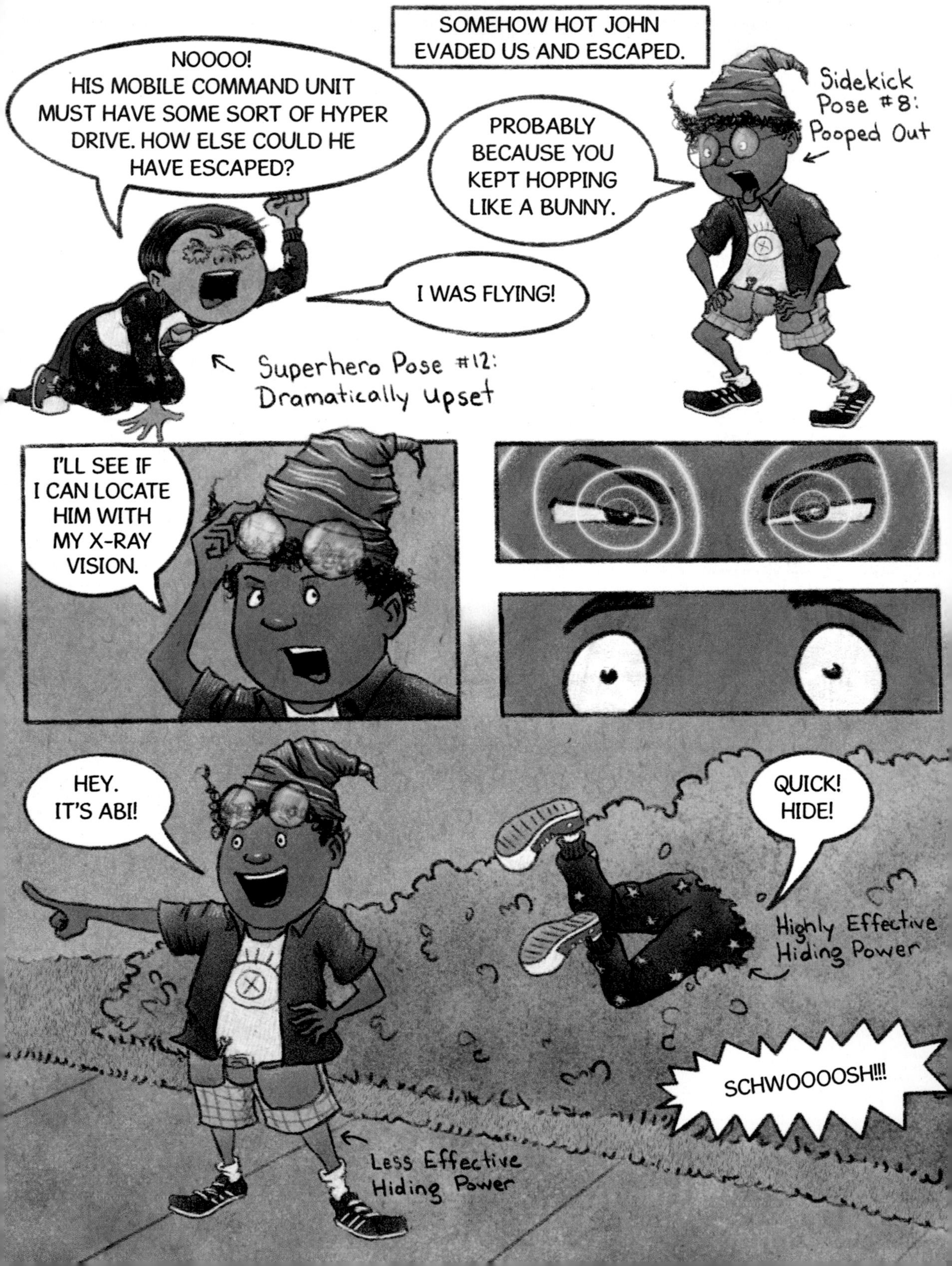
SOMEHOW HOT JOHN EVADED US AND ESCAPED.
NOOOO! HIS MOBILE COMMAND UNIT MUST HAVE SOME SORT OF HYPER DRIVE. HOW ELSE COULD HE HAVE ESCAPED?
PROBABLY BECAUSE YOU KEPT HOPPING LIKE A BUNNY.
Sidekick Pose #8: Pooped Out
I WAS FLYING!
Superhero Pose #12: Dramatically Upset
I'LL SEE IF I CAN LOCATE HIM WITH MY X-RAY VISION.
HEY. IT'S ABI!
QUICK! HIDE!
Highly Effective Hiding Power
SCHWOOOOSH!!!
Less Effective Hiding Power

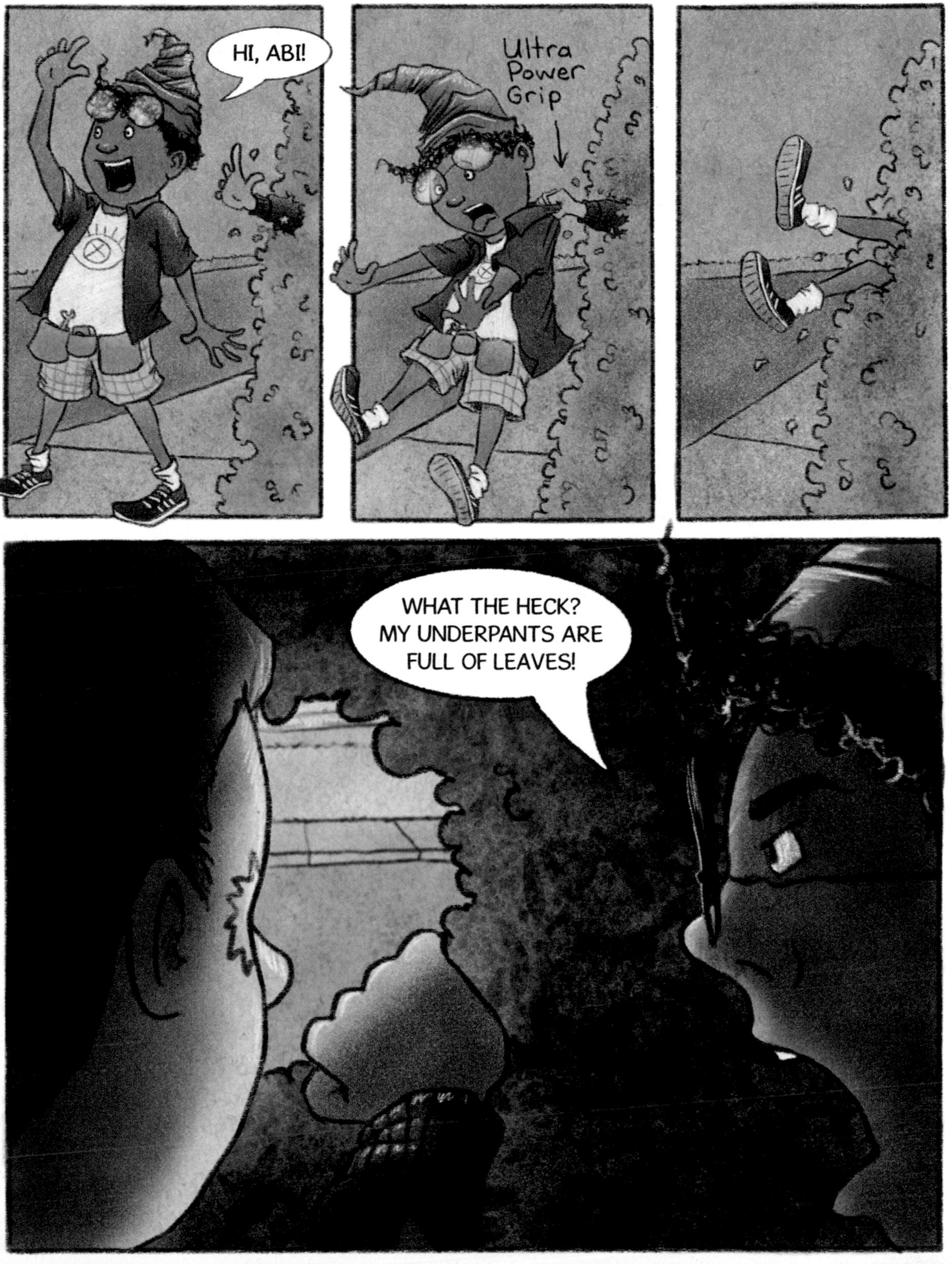
HI, ABI!
Ultra Power Grip
WHAT THE HECK? MY UNDERPANTS ARE FULL OF LEAVES!

Abi skipped up the other side of the street. She was pushing a toy stroller covered with a blanket and singing a song about cupcakes. She drew closer and closer to our hiding spot.

"I'm using my Quick-Change Chameleon Camouflage Power," I whispered in Rudy's ear. "Don't move and there's no way she'll be able to see us in here."

We held our breath as Abi skipped past our brilliant hiding spot.

"Hi, guys!" she sang. She waved excitedly and headed off down the street toward her own headquarters. The stroller squeaked and bounced over the cracks in the sidewalk.

"How did she see us?" I asked, stepping out of the bush and brushing leaves and twigs out of my hair. "With my Quick-Change Chameleon Camouflage Power, I blend in perfectly with my surroundings."

"I'd have to be wearing a blindfold not to see you," Abi called back over her shoulder. "You're standing in the bushes in your pajamas with a bright red pillowcase around your neck."

"Have you considered a better outfit?" Rudy asked. "One that doesn't make you look like a deranged toddler?"

"We have no time for that, young Rudy," I said. "My Brilliant Super Brain is occupied with more important matters. Like how we are going to catch a criminal genius like Hot John."

"Yeah," Rudy said. "You keep calling him a super-genius criminal, but I'm not so sure about that. Why would a super-genius use squirrels to help him with his plans? Squirrels are totally ridiculous. Why wouldn't a super-genius villain use some big, ferocious animal? Like lions? Or bears? Or a specially trained army of mutant, fire-breathing rhinoceroses? The more I think about it, the more I think that Hot John is pretty much the exact opposite of a supervillain. He drives around in a busted-up van and has fluffy little squirrels for his evil minions. He doesn't even have a cool villain outfit. He wears jeans and a faded old T-shirt with his phone number on it. What kind of villain goes around with his phone number on his shirt? It doesn't make any sense."

"We don't have time to make sense," I said. "This is action time!"

"Time is exactly what we don't have," Rudy said. "If we haven't found Cupcake before Miss Boyle gets home, then—"

"I know," I interrupted.

"And you won't get the—"

"I know."

"And Miss Boyle will—"

"I know!"

"And I get your—"

"I KNOW!" I cried, throwing my hands in the air. "This is getting desperate. We need more time if we're going to rescue Cupcake before Miss Boyle comes home."

I paced back and forth, my Super Brain struggling to come up with a brilliant plan.

"I've got it!" I cried. "We need more time, right? So, if we use our incredible powers to run fast enough, we can make time go backward. Then we can get to Miss Boyle's house before Hot John does. We'll be waiting there when Hot John arrives to kidnap Cupcake, and we can capture him. It's risky. Incredibly risky. But it's our only chance."

Rudy scratched his head. "Wait . . . What?"

"It's just like in issue #1128 of *Captain Fantastic*. Captain Fantastic goes to get a haircut, but he doesn't realize that the barber is actually his fourth worst arch-enemy, The Stylist, in disguise. The Stylist gives Captain Fantastic an awful haircut and all the other superheroes make fun of Captain Fantastic and it hurts his self-esteem. So he goes to the desert and runs so fast that he goes back in time to just before he got the haircut. Then, he goes to the barber shop and captures The Stylist and puts him in prison, where he's forced to give all the prisoners the same haircut every day for the rest of his life. It all makes perfect sense."

Rudy fidgeted with The Tape Measure of Truth. "No, dude. It does not. How does running fast make you go back in time?"

"It's very complicated," I explained, crouching into a Super Stretch so I wouldn't get a Power Cramp when we blasted through the time barrier. "It has to do with the space-time continuum. And sunspots. And, possibly, anti-matter. Ready?"

Rudy put the Tape Measure of Truth back in his toolbelt and adjusted his Wonder Goggles and the Cone of Brain Safety.™ He crouched down next to me. "Dude? What if we go back in time and meet ourselves and there are four of us instead of two of us?"

"Then we can help ourselves rescue Cupcake," I said. "It will be even easier! Let's go!"

We exploded down the street faster than laser beams with jet packs on them. . . .

AWAY TO JUSTICE!

YOU GET WHAT YOU GET AND YOU DON'T GET UPSET!

These Battle Cries Keep Getting Worse

← Super-Cool Speed Blast →

WE RACED FASTER AND FASTER. I COULD FEEL TIME BENDING AND THE VERY FABRIC OF THE UNIVERSE UNRAVELING.

AS WE APPROACHED THE SPEED OF LIGHT, I HEARD RUDY YELL OVER THE ROAR OF THE WIND.

I USED MY SPEED-PROOF BINOCU-VISION TO SCAN THE AREA.

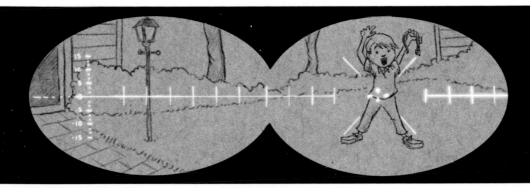

THE PARASITE STOOD ON HIS FRONT LAWN WAVING SOMETHING OVER HIS HEAD. I ZOOMED IN WITH MY AMAZE-O-VISION TO SEE WHAT IT WAS.

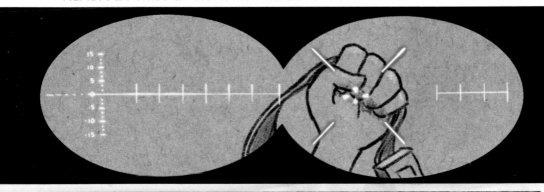

I SKIDDED TO A STOP WITH MY SPECTACULAR SUPER-STOPPING POWER.

Super Skid

"Freeze right there, Parasite," I cried, jumping up and landing in **SUPERHERO POSE #1: SUPERHEROIC**. "We caught you."

The Parasite's shoulders slumped. He sniffed a long, shuddering snork of air. He held up the object I had seen him holding.

Cupcake's PuppyVision collar.

"Cupcake is gone," The Parasite croaked.

Chapter 9

A CONFESSION

"We know Cupcake is gone, Parasite," I said in my deep, rich, heroic voice.

"Wait a minute," Rudy said, lifting his Wonder Goggles. "Where did you get Cupcake's PuppyVision Collar?"

Once again, my Deluxe Genius Brain Power immediately figured out what was happening. "YOU kidnapped Cupcake!"

"SHHHHH!!" The Parasite hissed.

"Do not shoosh me, you foul villain! You kidnapped Cupcake!" I yelled. "Give her back right now!"

He looked like he was about to cry.

Or throw up.

Or both.

He reared his head back and groaned. I quickly stepped away so I wouldn't get puke on my Hyper-Drive Sneakers.

But The Parasite didn't puke. And he didn't lunge at me and attack me. He took a deep breath and wiped at his eyes.

"Yes," he whispered, looking back at his fortress. "I took Cupcake."

"I knew it!" I cried. "I knew it was you all along!"

"No, you didn't," Rudy said, poking me in the arm. "First you thought mutant, brainwashed squirrels kidnapped Cupcake. Then you thought The Mystery Neighbors kidnapped Cupcake. Then you thought Hot John kidnapped Cupcake using mutant brainwashed squirrels. You never once said anything about Chaz."

"The point is, I have caught the evil criminal. Now we will take Cupcake home before Miss Boyle arrives. Miss Boyle will be happy, I will collect my money, and you will not get that rare first edition of *Captain Fantastic*, Parasite. I will. And I will become the greatest superhero the world has ever known. And you will go to jail. Now give Cupcake back immediately."

The Parasite heaved a giant sob and hung his head. "No."

"So," I growled, stepping forward. "You're going to make this tough on yourself, huh, Parasite? Not going to give up Cupcake without a fight? Well, all right. Prepare yourself for . . ." I jumped into the air and landed in **SUPERHERO POSE #25: ABOUT TO GET INTO A HUGE AND SPECTACULAR FIGHT WITH LOTS OF AWESOME SPECIAL EFFECTS AND EXPLOSIONS AND STUFF.**

76

Rudy jumped up next to me.

"Away to Justice!" I yelled.

"That's the way the cookie crumbles!" Rudy yelled.

The Parasite stepped away from our amazing display of heroic awesomeness. "No!" he hissed again, looking back toward his evil fortress. "No! Be quiet! I don't have Cupcake. I told you. She's gone."

"We know she's gone, Parasite. We've already been through this. You told us you took her. Now you're saying that you didn't. The time for talking is over. And I'm running out of time. So now it's time for . . . ACTION!"

I launched myself at The Parasite with my **MILLION-MEGAWATT SUPER-DOUBLE HYPER KICK**. . . .

One million megawatts of AWESOME!

HE MUST HAVE SOME KIND OF EVIL FORCE-FIELD DEVICE. I FELL TO THE GROUND AND THE PARASITE ESCAPED!

I JUMPED TO MY FEET AND CHASED THE FLEEING EVILDOER.

THE PARASITE RACED STRAIGHT TOWARD MY HEADQUARTERS. WHO KNEW WHAT SORT OF DIABOLICAL MAYHEM HE WAS PLANNING? I HAD TO STOP HIM.

MY EXTEND-O-ARMS WERE UNABLE TO REACH HIM. I HAD ONLY ONE LAST HOPE TO MAKE HIM STOP.

"I've frozen you and now I have complete control of your mind, Parasite," I told him.

"No, you don't," he gasped, yanking his arms free from the Unbreakable Titanium Grip of Steel that I had on him.

"I made you run right to my headquarters with my Mind Control Powers," I explained, pointing to my high-security fortress.

"No, you didn't," he said. "I came here so I could tell you what happened to Cupcake without my parents hearing."

"So, tell us," Rudy said, lifting his Wonder Goggles. "Don't make me use the Tape Measure of Truth on you, Parasite."

He lifted the tape measure from his toolbelt and pulled a few feet of the tape out.

"Put it away, Rudy," I said. "We don't need to resort to violence. Yet."

Rudy sighed and stuck it back into his toolbelt.

"So, where's Cupcake, Parasite?" I growled. "We're running out of time, and you're running out of . . . my . . . patience."

"What?" Rudy asked. "That didn't make any sense. What are you trying to—"

"I told you," The Parasite interrupted. He ran his fingers through his sweaty hair. "I took Cupcake, all right? I was trying to keep you from getting the money from Miss Boyle so you couldn't buy the comic book on Monday. I was walking by her house and heard her offer to give you $100 to watch her yappy little dog. I need that *Captain Fantastic* comic book. I have every issue except that one. I have to have it to complete my collection.

"So I took Cupcake from her house when you went to Rudy's house. I brought her to my house and tied her to a tree in the shade. Then I went and got some dog food for her."

"That's why you had dog food before," Rudy said. "And that's how you knew that Cupcake was missing!"

"So, where's Cupcake now?" I asked.

"I don't know," The Parasite wailed. "That's what I've been trying to tell you. I got back to my house with the dog food and she was gone. All I found was this, lying on the ground." He held up Cupcake's PuppyVision collar. "If my dad finds out that I took Cupcake and lost her, he's going to kill me. He's always talking about not doing anything to reflect badly on the Pharsight name. That's why I had to run here so we could talk about it. If he finds out what happened, I'm a dead man. You guys have to help me."

"Why should we help you?" Rudy asked. "You took Cupcake in the first place. This is all your fault."

"I know," The Parasite whined. "But if my dad finds out, I'm going to be in huge trouble."

"Personally, I'm okay with that," Rudy said.

"No, Rudy," I said, laying a hand on his shoulder. "That's not The Superhero Way. As superheroes, we must be willing to help anyone. Even a loathsome, foul, cruel-hearted criminal like The Parasite. And we cannot risk upsetting poor Miss Boyle."

"I'm not a criminal, Mr. Running-Around-Town-in-His-Little-Pajamas," The Parasite said. "And if we don't find Cupcake, Miss Boyle will be a million times madder than my dad will be. I'll get in big trouble, but you two will be dead meat."

We were standing there in silence contemplating our impending doom when The Chief poked her head out the front door of my headquarters.

"Stevie? Stevie, sweetie? You have a phone call. It's Miss Boyle."

Chapter 10

FRENCH PRESIDENTS AND SOME BAD NEWS. SOME VERY BAD NEWS.

I hated to deceive The Chief, but I had no choice. I engaged my Quick-Change Chameleon Camouflage Power and used my Voice-Disguising Power so The Chief wouldn't know it was me.

"Stevie eez not heeeerrrr," I called out in a perfect imitation of the President of France. "Pleez leave a message at zee beep. BEEP!"

"Stevie," The Chief said. "I can see you standing right there behind my begonias. In your pajamas. Come get the phone and stop fooling around. Miss Boyle wants to talk to you."

"We're sorry," I called out in a perfect imitation of a robot, "All of our customer service representatives are busy at this time. Please try your call—"

"Now!" The Chief hissed, holding the phone out toward me.

I took a deep, heroic breath and marched over to the phone.

"Here he is, Heather," The Chief said into the phone before handing it to me.

"She's calling about Cupcake," The Chief whispered to me.

The
Chief

I took the phone.

"Hello, citizen," I said in my calmest, deepest, most heroic voice.

"Ohhhhhhh, Stevie!" squealed Miss Boyle. "How is my little poochie smookums? I miss my wittle baby soooooo much! Is everything all right? Did you read the entire binder? Has she had her midday paw rub yet? If she doesn't have it, her adorable little footsies get sore and that makes mama's baby puppy schnookums all cranky wanky."

"Ummm . . ." I gulped.

"And did you remember to cut her lunch up into very small pieces? Too much chewing tires her out, and I'm afraid that she'll choke if she eats while she's tired."

"Ummm . . ." I gulped again.

"And remember that my little snuggie-wuggums needs to have her imported mineral water served at 76 degrees, exactly. Otherwise she might get a tummy cramp. And she likes it with a small twist of lime in it. Not lemon! Only lime. Lemon gives her acid reflux. Ooooh, I miss her so, so, so, so much. I should be at the bakery soon. I stopped to get gas on the way and the battery in my van died and I had to wait for a tow truck to jump-start me so I'm running a bit late. I'll grab the cake and then I'll be on my way home."

"Ummm . . ." I gulped.

She was running late! That meant that we had some extra time to find Cupcake.

"Oh, it looks like there's some traffic ahead. I'd better hang up. I don't like to talk and drive."

"Okay," I managed to squeak.

"Oh, wait!" Miss Boyle squealed. "Before I hang up, put my little furry babykins on the phone so mama can say hello to her."

"Wha . . .?" I croaked.

"Let me say hello to my little pookie-pie. Put Cupcake on the phone for me, Stevie."

"I . . . uhhh . . . ummm . . ."

I cupped my hand over the phone to block my voice. . . .

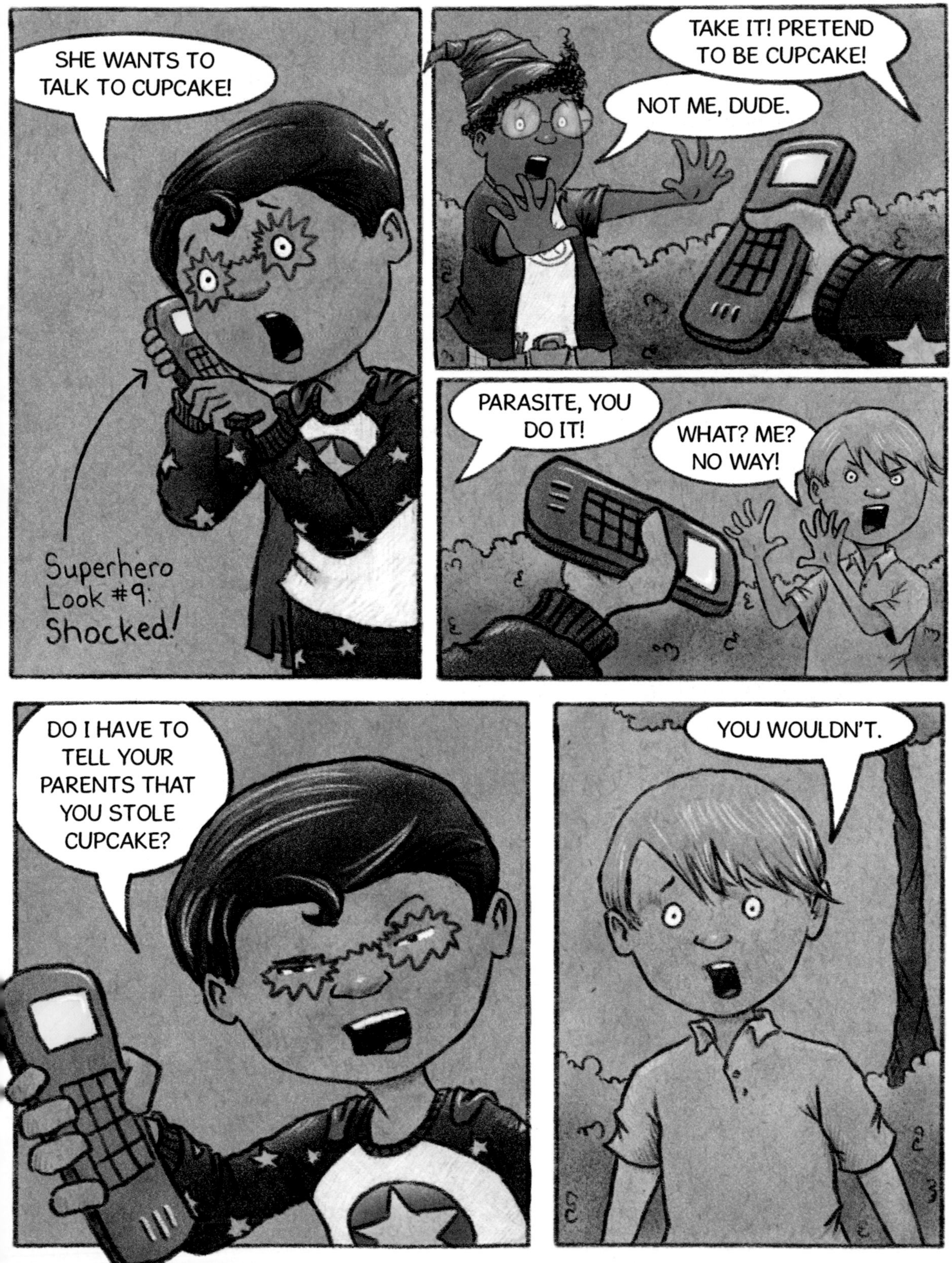
SHE WANTS TO TALK TO CUPCAKE!
Superhero Look #9: Shocked!
TAKE IT! PRETEND TO BE CUPCAKE!
NOT ME, DUDE.
PARASITE, YOU DO IT!
WHAT? ME? NO WAY!
DO I HAVE TO TELL YOUR PARENTS THAT YOU STOLE CUPCAKE?
YOU WOULDN'T.

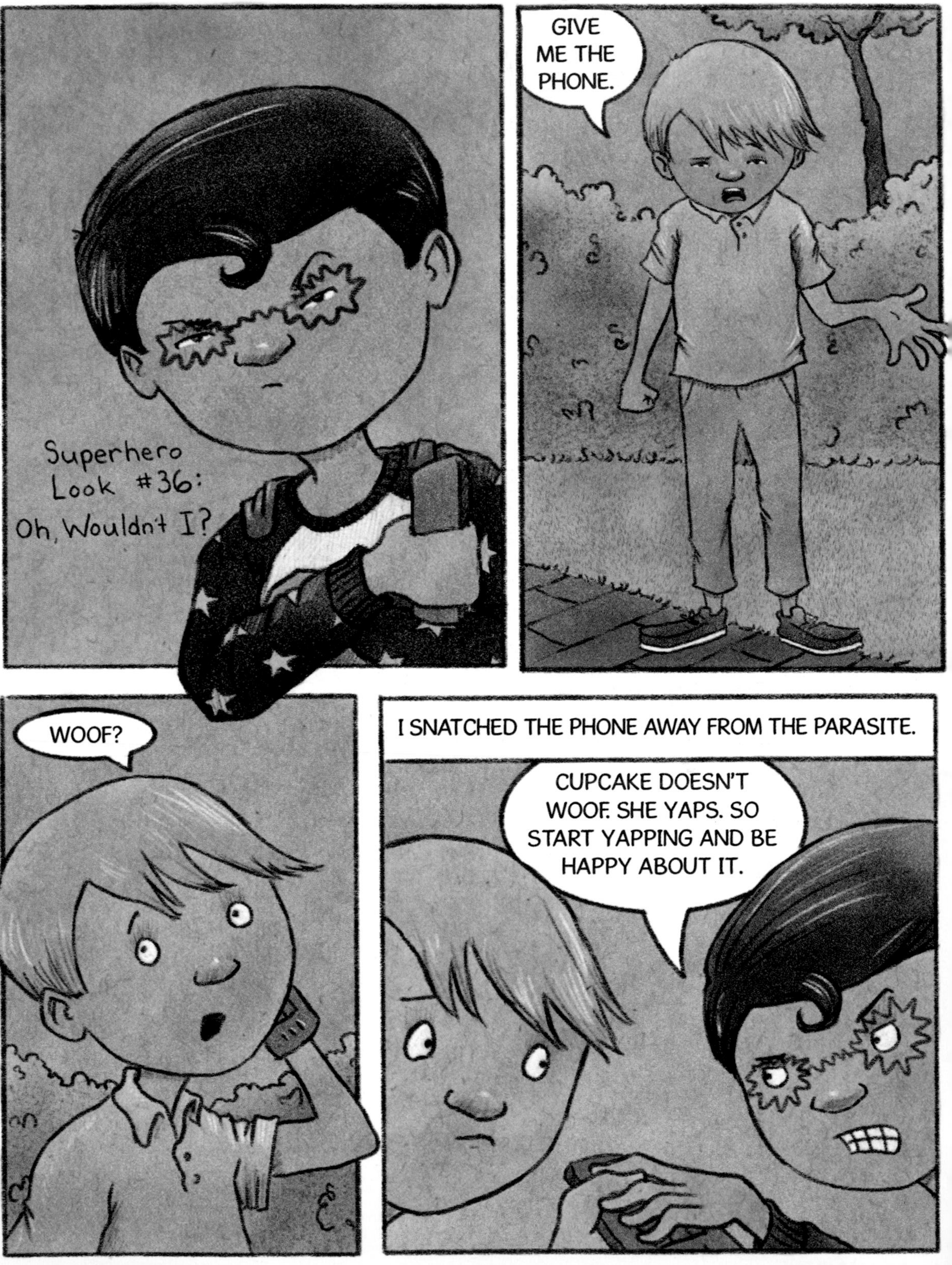
Superhero Look #36: Oh, Wouldn't I?
GIVE ME THE PHONE.
WOOF?
I SNATCHED THE PHONE AWAY FROM THE PARASITE.
CUPCAKE DOESN'T WOOF. SHE YAPS. SO START YAPPING AND BE HAPPY ABOUT IT.

"Here she is, Miss Boyle," I said into the phone.

I handed it back to The Parasite. He looked like he was going to throw up again.

The Parasite held the phone up to his ear and gulped. "Yip? Yap? Whuff! Bar-bar-bar-barrrrrr! Yip yip yip yip yip yip yip!" He dragged in a slobbering breath that sounded impressively like Cupcake drooling her foul, toxic drool.

The Parasite ended the call with a wet, slobbery yowl and handed the phone back to me.

"See Miss Boyle? She's as happy as a puppy could be."

I listened as Miss Boyle talked even faster than normal.

"Uh-huh," I said. "No . . . I . . . But . . . Okay, Miss Boyle."

I hung the phone up.

"What did she say, Stevie?" asked The Parasite, wiping drool from his chin.

"Stevie?" Rudy asked, waving his hand in front of my eyes a few times. "Stevie? Are you in there?" He snapped his fingers in my face.

"Hello? Stevie? What did Miss Boyle say?"

I looked from Rudy to The Parasite.

"She said that she thought Cupcake didn't sound good," I groaned. "She's worried that Cupcake might be getting sick. Miss Boyle is turning around and coming right home. She'll be here in an hour."

Chapter 11

SPEAKING WITH THE ENEMY.

"Parasite," I announced, "we're going to have to work together if we have any hope of rescuing Cupcake. I don't like you, and you don't like me—"

"And I don't really like him very much, either," The Parasite interrupted, pointing at Rudy.

"Thanks, Chaz," Rudy said, rolling his X-Ray eyes.

"Well, I guess it's not just that I don't like you guys," The Parasite said. "It's also that you're really, really annoying. I mean, look at yourselves. Running around the neighborhood in those goofy costumes, pretending that you can fly and—"

"Like I was saying," I interrupted. "You were the last one to see Cupcake. We're going to have to work together to save her. Plus, if you don't help us, your dad will kill you. This is just like issue #444 of *Captain Fantastic*. The one where Captain Fantastic is held captive on—"

"The Planet of The Baritone Women!" The Parasite chimed in, his eyes lighting up. "And they want him to sing tenor in their upcoming production of—"

"*The Sound of Music!*" I cried. "But they also captured his arch-enemy, The Stinkfish, who actually has a pleasing alto voice. And they keep both of them—"

"Locked in the backstage prison until they learn their lines!" the Parasite yelped, flapping his hands. "And if they mess up their lines, they'll be killed by a raving mob of zombie assassin theater critics. So the only way they can learn their lines is by . . ."

"Working together!" The Parasite and I both yelled.

"It all makes perfect sense," I said, pacing across the grass. "If we work together, we can rescue Cupcake before Miss Boyle gets home. We have an hour."

"Less than an hour, now," Rudy said. "Because you two just wasted a bunch of time talking about Captain Fantastic singing a song with his arch-enemy."

I leaped over the security gate and onto the sidewalk. "Away to Justice!"

"The Early Bird Gets the Worm!" Rudy yelled.

The three of us stood on the sidewalk in perfect battle formation.

Ready for action.

Sidekick Pose #7: Check Out My Gadgets

Superhero Pose #4: Let's Get Ready to Rumble!

Non-Superhero Pose #1: Looking Like A Weirdo

Ready for anything.

"So, um, now what?" The Parasite asked. "My legs are getting sore from standing like this. Shouldn't we actually be looking for Cupcake instead of just posing in the street like this?"

Rudy lifted his Wonder Goggles and scanned the area.

"Well, X?" I asked. "What have you got to report?"

"I don't see Cupcake," Rudy reported.

The Parasite sighed. "What is wrong with you two? We can't just stand here, waiting for the kidnapper to show up. He's not going to just—"

"Hey! It's Hot John!" Rudy cried, pointing down the street.

Hot John's mobile command unit pulled around the corner. . . .

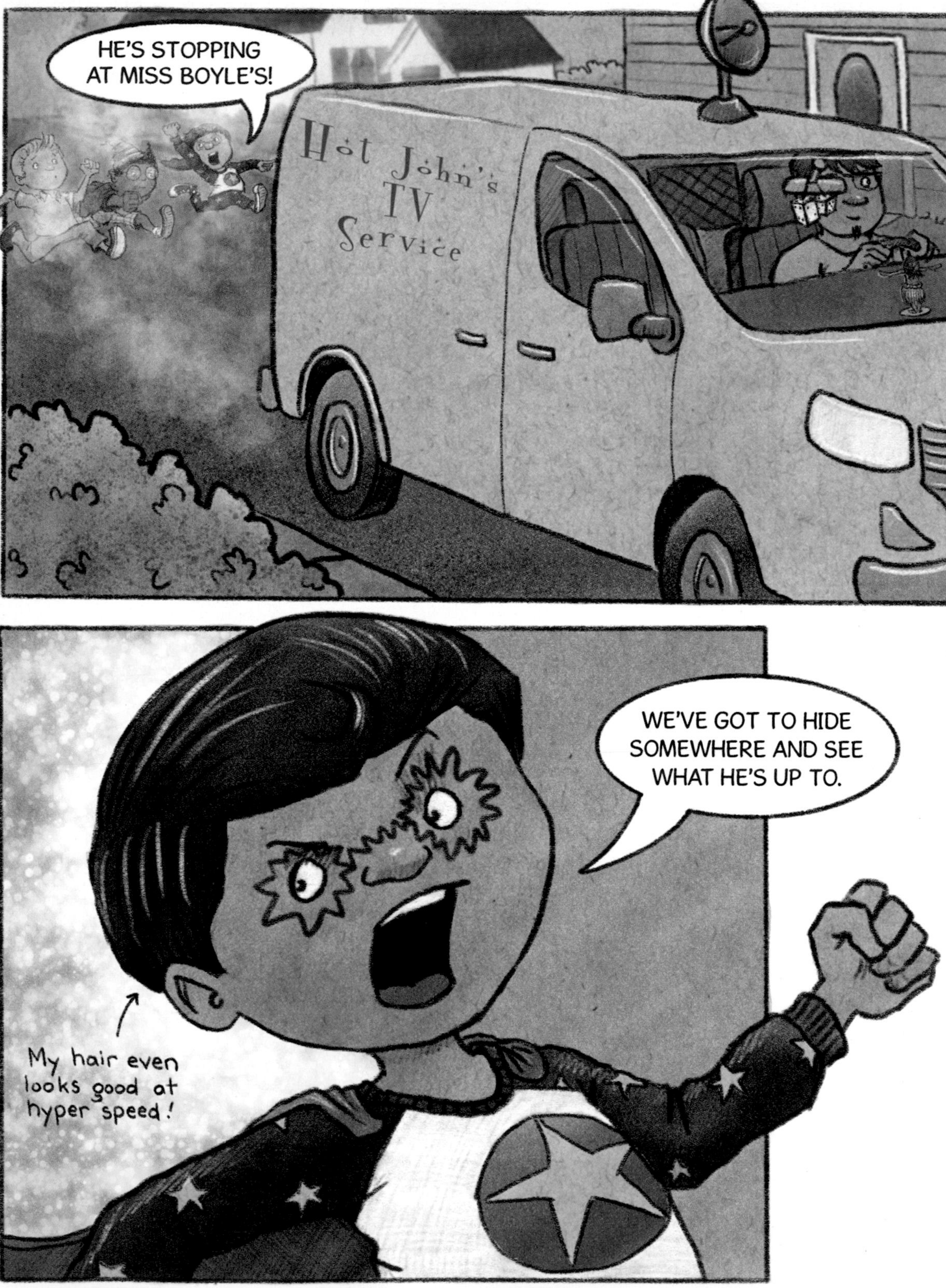
HE'S STOPPING AT MISS BOYLE'S!
Hot John's TV Service
WE'VE GOT TO HIDE SOMEWHERE AND SEE WHAT HE'S UP TO.
My hair even looks good at hyper speed!

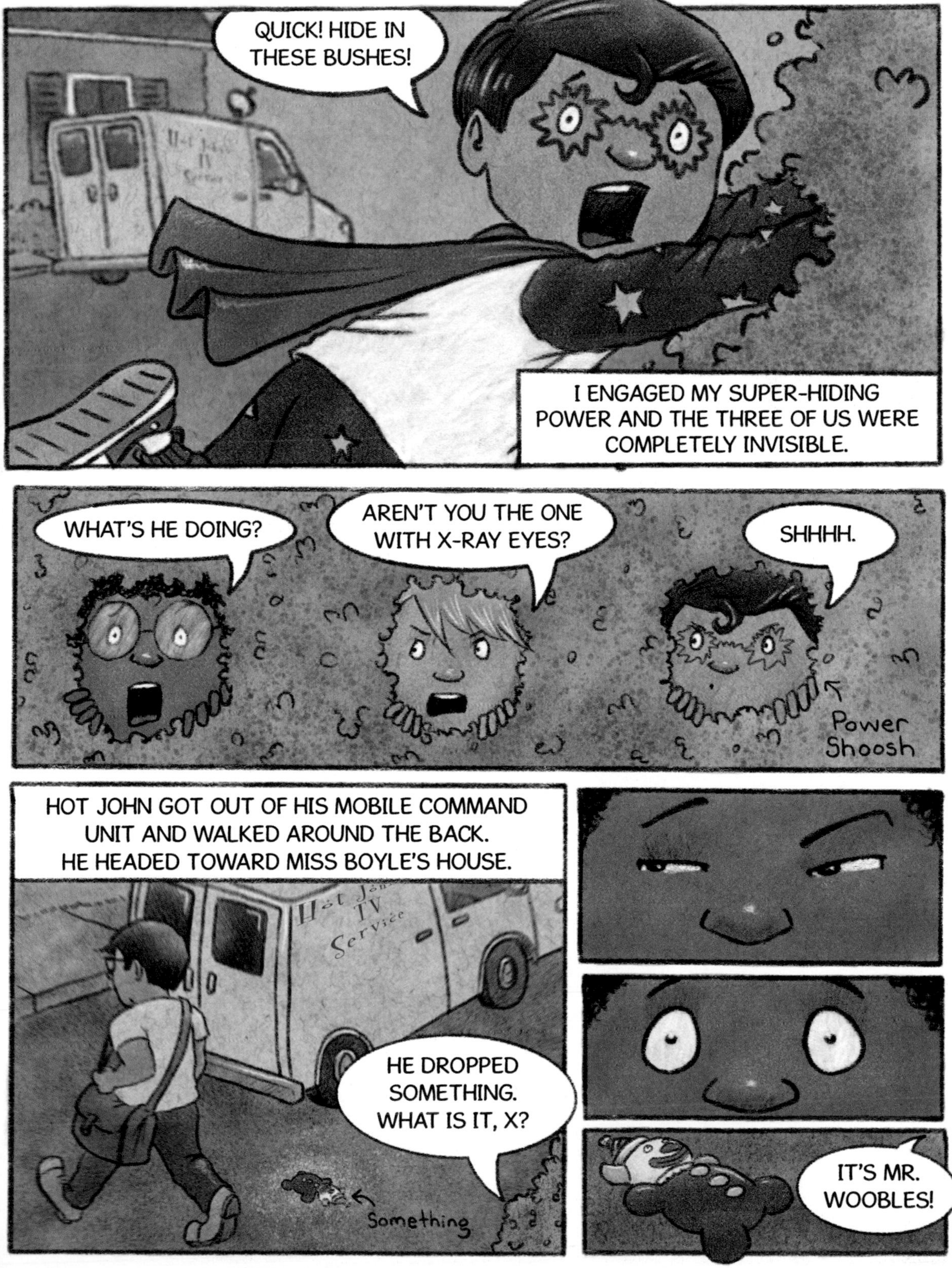
QUICK! HIDE IN THESE BUSHES!
I ENGAGED MY SUPER-HIDING POWER AND THE THREE OF US WERE COMPLETELY INVISIBLE.
WHAT'S HE DOING?
AREN'T YOU THE ONE WITH X-RAY EYES?
SHHHH.
Power Shoosh
HOT JOHN GOT OUT OF HIS MOBILE COMMAND UNIT AND WALKED AROUND THE BACK. HE HEADED TOWARD MISS BOYLE'S HOUSE.
HE DROPPED SOMETHING. WHAT IS IT, X?
Something
IT'S MR. WOOBLES!

Chapter 12

A NEW ARCH-ENEMY. AGAIN.

"Looks like we found our kidnapper," I said.

Rudy shook his head. "I don't get it. This doesn't make any sense. Chaz is the kidnapper. Why would Hot John take Cupcake from Chaz?"

"Oh, it does make sense, young Rudy," I said, patting his head.

Rudy swatted my hand away. "Stop calling me 'Young Rudy.' I'm four months older than you. And don't pat my head or I'll break your fingers with my X-Ray Karate Chop."

"What the heck is an X-Ray Karate Chop?" Chaz asked. "That doesn't even make any sense. How can a karate chop be X-Ray? If you—"

"This is just like issue #57 of *The Jeweler*," I interrupted. "The one where The Jeweler is hired to make a necklace for the The Queen of Europe, but his arch-enemy, Cubic Zircon, disguises himself as a messenger and distracts The Jeweler with a fake letter from The Queen. While The Jeweler is reading the letter, Cubic Zircon replaces the necklace for the Queen with an exact duplicate that he made. Except that his has a secret mind-control device in it that he's going to use on The Queen of Europe. It all makes perfect sense."

"Of course!" The Parasite agreed. "It's just like that!"

"That makes no sense at all!" Rudy groaned.

"Think about it," I explained. "Hot John must have kidnapped Cupcake using his Brainwave Amplification—"

"This isn't about the squirrels again, is it?" Rudy sighed. "Enough with the squirrels."

"No, no, no," I said. "I was wrong about the squirrels. Somebody else must be controlling them. But I know that Hot John kidnapped Cupcake, and I've got all the proof I need right here."

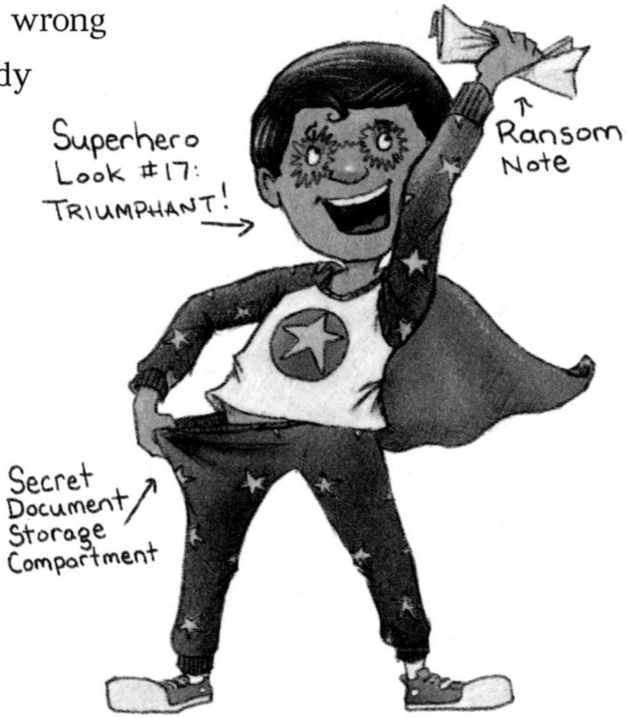
Superhero Look #17: TRIUMPHANT!
Ransom Note
Secret Document Storage Compartment

I pulled the ransom note from my secret document storage compartment.

"Why do you have an envelope stuffed into your underpants, you freak?" The Parasite asked. "That's so unsanitary!"

"My Super Suit doesn't have any pockets," I explained. "This 'bill' that Hot John gave us to deliver isn't a bill at all. It's a decoy. He gave it to us to deliver to get us out of the way. Hot John knew that Cupcake was at The Parasite's evil lair all along."

"It's actually a small mansion, not an evil lair," The Parasite corrected. "You can tell because we have fountains and nice landscaping."

I sighed and continued. "And Hot John gave us this 'bill' to deliver to make sure that we were out of the way when he drove over to The Parasite's lair—"

"Mansion," The Parasite corrected.

"—to kidnap Cupcake!"

Rudy shook his head. "So he used the bill to get us out of the way. Okay. That actually makes sense. But how did Hot John know that Cupcake was at Chaz's—"

"Mansion," finished The Parasite.

"With this!" I cried, snatching the PuppyVision collar from The Parasite's hand.

"With a TV remote control?" Rudy asked.

I waved the PuppyVision collar in the air. "This is no simple remote control, Rudy," I explained. "It's just like the fake necklace in *The Jeweler.* Hot John told us that it could read the wearer's brain waves. Hot John must be able to use it in reverse to control Cupcake's mind and make her come right to him.

"Think about it! When Hot John installs PuppyVision, the owners willingly strap a mind-control collar around their dog's neck. One that Hot John can use to make the dog come to him. Then he can hold the dog for ransom. He can do that to dog owners all over the world and become rich. It's brilliant!

"And the controls for all his evil collars must be in there." I pointed to Hot John's mobile command unit. "He cleverly disguises himself as a TV installation guy, and his victims actually pay him to come steal their dogs."

"That's why he has his name and phone number on his shirt!" Rudy cried.

"If all his stuff is in there," The Parasite said, "then Cupcake must be in there, too! I'm going to look. Cover me!"

"Parasite! Wait!" I said. He marched right over to Hot John's mobile command unit and climbed up onto the back bumper to look in the window.

"Whoa . . ." he gasped.

Rudy and I ran over to him.

"What is it?" I asked.

"It's Mr. Woobles!" The Parasite cried.

"What are you talking about?" I asked, jumping up on the bumper next to him.

The Parasite pointed through the window. "Right there. See? It's Mr. Woobles!"

I peered through the window with my Ultra-Mega Binocu-Vision; and there, amid spools of wire and buckets of evil looking electronic devices, sat Mr. Woobles.

"I thought Hot John dropped Mr. Woobles on the street," I said, turning to Rudy.

"He did," Rudy said, grabbing Mr. Woobles from the street.

Rudy kept a lookout with his X-Ray Vision while The Parasite opened the back door of the van and grabbed the second Mr. Woobles. It was a perfect match of Cupcake's favorite chew toy except that it didn't look all chewed up like it had before.

The Parasite gave Mr. Woobles a gentle squeeze.

My Deluxe Genius Super Brain Power immediately figured out Hot John's scheme. "Hot John is creating an army of Mr. Woobles clones to help him in his quest to kidnap all the dogs in the world. He knows how much dogs love squeaky chew toys. It's just like in issue #550 of *Commander Beefy*, when Commander Beefy discovers that his arch-enemy, Dr. Mayo, has created an evil army of living Tater Tots to help him take over the world. It all makes perfect sense."

"Commander Beefy? Dr. Mayo? Evil Tater Tots? That. Makes. No. Sense. At. All. And . . . uh-oh . . ." Rudy groaned. He pointed toward Miss Boyle's house. "Hot John is coming."

Chapter 13

ACTION! AND DUCT TAPE!

I used my Silent-Stealth Sneak Power to duck around the side of the vehicle with Rudy. My Quick-Change Chameleon Camouflage Power instantly made us completely invisible to the human eye. The Parasite quietly closed the door of Hot John's command unit and slipped around the side just as Hot John appeared at the end of Miss Boyle's driveway.

"I didn't get a chance to see the whole interior," The Parasite whispered. "Cupcake must be locked away in a hidden compartment."

Hot John walked across the street toward us.

"He's coming," Rudy whispered. "Do something!"

"I've already got a plan," I said. "This is just like issue #750 of *Man-Bear* when Man-Bear was stalking his arch-enemy, The Ring Master, who was trying to catch him so he could display him in his evil Circus of Death. The Ring Master set a trap for Man-Bear and Man-Bear fell into it. It all makes perfect sense."

Rudy stared at me. "And then what?" he whispered.

"And then nothing," I said. "The Ring Master caught him and used him as an exhibit in his evil circus. That was the last issue of that comic book. It's a very valuable collector's item."

"I have a copy of that one," The Parasite said with a nasty smirk. "It's worth more than a new washing machine."

"A new washing machine?" Rudy asked. "What kind of comparison is that? How much does a new washing machine cost?"

"It totally depends on the features," The Parasite explained. "Ours is the deluxe model, so it has a fancy dirt detecting sys—"

I shooshed them with a Power Shoosh.

I pointed toward Hot John, who was digging his keys out of his pocket.

We crouched silently as he opened the back doors and climbed in. I engaged my Super Stealthy Mode and the three of us crept up behind Hot John completely undetected.

"Now's our chance," I whispered. "We can trap him."

I pointed to Rudy's toolbelt.

He reached in and pulled out the Duct Tape of Justice. "This?" he whispered.

I sprang into action. . . .

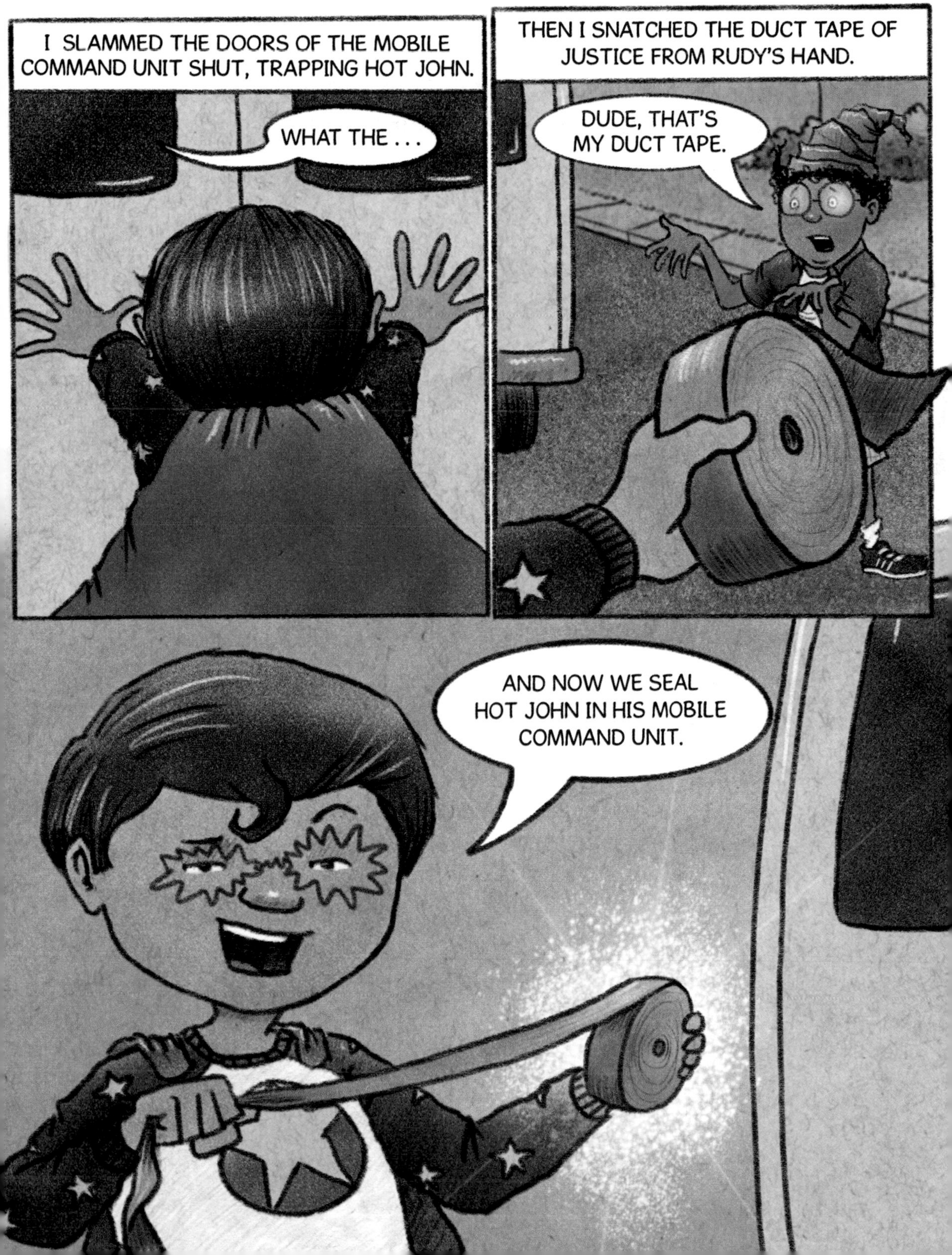
I SLAMMED THE DOORS OF THE MOBILE COMMAND UNIT SHUT, TRAPPING HOT JOHN.
WHAT THE . . .
THEN I SNATCHED THE DUCT TAPE OF JUSTICE FROM RUDY'S HAND.
DUDE, THAT'S MY DUCT TAPE.
AND NOW WE SEAL HOT JOHN IN HIS MOBILE COMMAND UNIT.

RUDY PULLED THE 11 mm WRENCH OF RETRIBUTION OUT OF HIS TOOL BELT.

HE SLID THE WRENCH THROUGH THE DOOR HANDLES, LOCKING THEM.

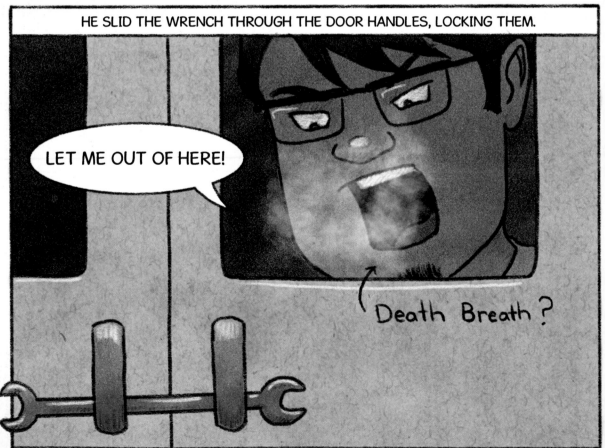

HOT JOHN WAS NOT HAPPY.

LET ME OUT!

BOOM!

A THUNDEROUS CRASH SHOOK THE VAN.

THE PARASITE GRABBED THE DUCT TAPE OF JUSTICE FROM ME.

WE NEED MORE DUCT TAPE TO HOLD HIM.

Duct Tape of Justice

HE RAN AROUND AND AROUND THE VAN SECURING ALL THE DOORS.

THE VILLAIN WAS TRAPPED.

I STOOD BACK TO INSPECT OUR WORK

← Superhero Pose #5: Slightly Smug

LOOKS LIKE HOT JOHN ISN'T SUCH . . . *HOT STUFF.*

I GUESS WE . . . *COOLED OFF* HOT JOHN.

MISS BOYLE'S CRUISING VESSEL SLOWLY ROUNDED THE CORNER. SHE WAS HOME.

Chapter 14

WE SHOULD HAVE USED MORE DUCT TAPE.

There was tremendous crash from inside Hot John's vehicle. "He's trying to escape!" I cried. "We've got to alert Miss Boyle to the danger and find a way to neutralize Hot John's powers!"

"What are Hot John's powers?" Rudy asked.

"I don't know," I admitted. "We'll have to figure that out as we go!"

We raced across the street and skidded to a stop behind Miss Boyle's cruising vessel. Except for Rudy. He kept right on running and crashed into the back of it.

Miss Boyle swung her door open and cried "Oh, Rudy! Are you okay? What are you boys doing? And why are you still in your pajamas, Stevie? Where's my little Cupcake?"

Sidekick Pose #13: Dazed and Confused

105

Rudy stood up and rubbed his head. "Oh, yeah. I'm okay, Miss Boyle. I'm an indestructible superhero."

He staggered over to the lawn and sat down, still rubbing his head.

"And . . ." I began, stepping forward to make our great announcement.

"We caught a super criminal!" The Parasite announced. "He was here leaving a ransom note for Cupcake, but we trapped him in his van."

"A ransom note for Cupcake?" Miss Boyle cried, her eyes growing wide. "What happened? Where is she?"

I cleared my throat, put my hands on my hips, and tilted my head slightly upward. "You needn't worry, citizen," I announced. "The Super Guys have the situation under control. It seems that while I was summoning my sidekick, Rudy—"

"I'm not your sidekick," Rudy interrupted. "I'm a superhero, too."

"It seems that as I was summoning my associate, Rudy—"

"And my superhero name is X, not Rudy."

"Where's Cupcake?" Miss Boyle pleaded, tears welling up in her fudgy brown eyes.

"As I was saying," I continued. "While I was out getting X to help me guard Cupcake, our arch-enemy, The Parasite, snuck over here and took the dog back to his evil lair—"

"It's actually a small mansion," The Parasite interrupted.

"—in an effort to prevent us from collecting the $100 reward and purchasing a special, rare collector's edition of the first issue of *Captain Fantastic* that I absolutely have to have if I am going to become an incredible superhero. Meanwhile, the evil super-genius villain Hot John distracted us by asking us to deliver a decoy ransom note disguised as a bill to your house while he used his terrible mind-control satellite unit to take control of Cupcake's brain using her PuppyVision collar and a clone of Mr. Woobles. He forced Cupcake to come to him so he could hold her for ransom as part of his devious, evil plan to take over the world by kidnapping everybody's dogs." I took a deep breath and nodded. "It all makes perfect sense."

Miss Boyle stared blankly for a minute, her big, brown eyes glistening like a melting chocolate chip.

"Where is Cupcake?" Miss Boyle wailed.

"Uh, dudes," Rudy said, standing up and pointing across the street. "Maybe you can ask *him*."

We all turned to see a very angry Hot John climbing out the driver's door window of his Evil Dog-napping Mobile.

Chapter 15

THE BIG FIGHT SCENE. SORT OF.

Hot John stormed across the street. "What the heck do you think you're doing?"

"Where is Cupcake?" wailed Miss Boyle again. "What happened to my little sweetie-pie?"

The Parasite whimpered and covered his face with his hands in a weak attempt to become invisible.

I jumped into **AWESOME SUPERHERO POSE #397: READY FOR THE BIG FIGHT SCENE**.

Rudy tried to do the same, but he tripped and

teetered for a minute before sprawling back onto the lawn.

Hot John marched right up to me and pointed an evil finger in my face. I ducked in case a gigantic fireball shot out of it. I still had no idea what kind of powers my arch-enemy had. "Why did you lock me in my van?"

The Parasite squeaked and stepped behind Miss Boyle, who was climbing out of her cruising vessel.

Rudy curled up into a ball on the lawn.

I put my hands on my hips and gave Hot John **SUPERHERO LOOK #8: DRAMATICALLY ARCHED EYEBROW**.

"We didn't lock you in your van. We used The Duct Tape of Justice to secure you in your Evil Mobile. And now the game is over, Hot John. Give Cupcake back to Miss Boyle."

"You have Cupcake?" Miss Boyle asked Hot John.

Hot John glared at me. "What the heck are you talking about?"

"I'm the one asking the questions here, Hot John." I pointed at him with my Iron Power Death Finger. "What have you done with Cupcake?"

"I'm here to deliver a bill for the PuppyVision I installed this morning," he cried.

"You asked us to deliver the bill. Or should I say the ransom note?" I said, waving the envelope in the air and

holding up the PuppyVision
Mind-Control Collar. "You
used this evil mind-control
collar to take control of
Cupcake's mind and force her
into captivity so you could
collect a huge ransom from
Miss Boyle!"

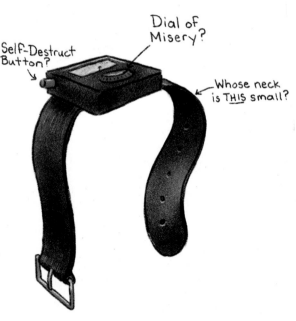

Hot John ran a hand
through his hair. "I gave you a
bill to deliver earlier," he said.
"Then I thought that maybe
you two might not be the
most reliable people for the job. I went into my van to
grab my bag and the next thing I know, you slammed the
doors shut and taped them closed."

"Because we're superheroes," Rudy said, standing up
again. "And you're our arch-enemy, even if you do have a
terrible supervillain name, a sad excuse for a vehicle, and
an awful supervillain outfit. And we caught you. So we win,
dude. Hand over the doggy."

"Will somebody please tell me what's happening here?"
Miss Boyle sobbed. "Where is Cupcake?"

I took a deep breath and cleared my throat. . . .

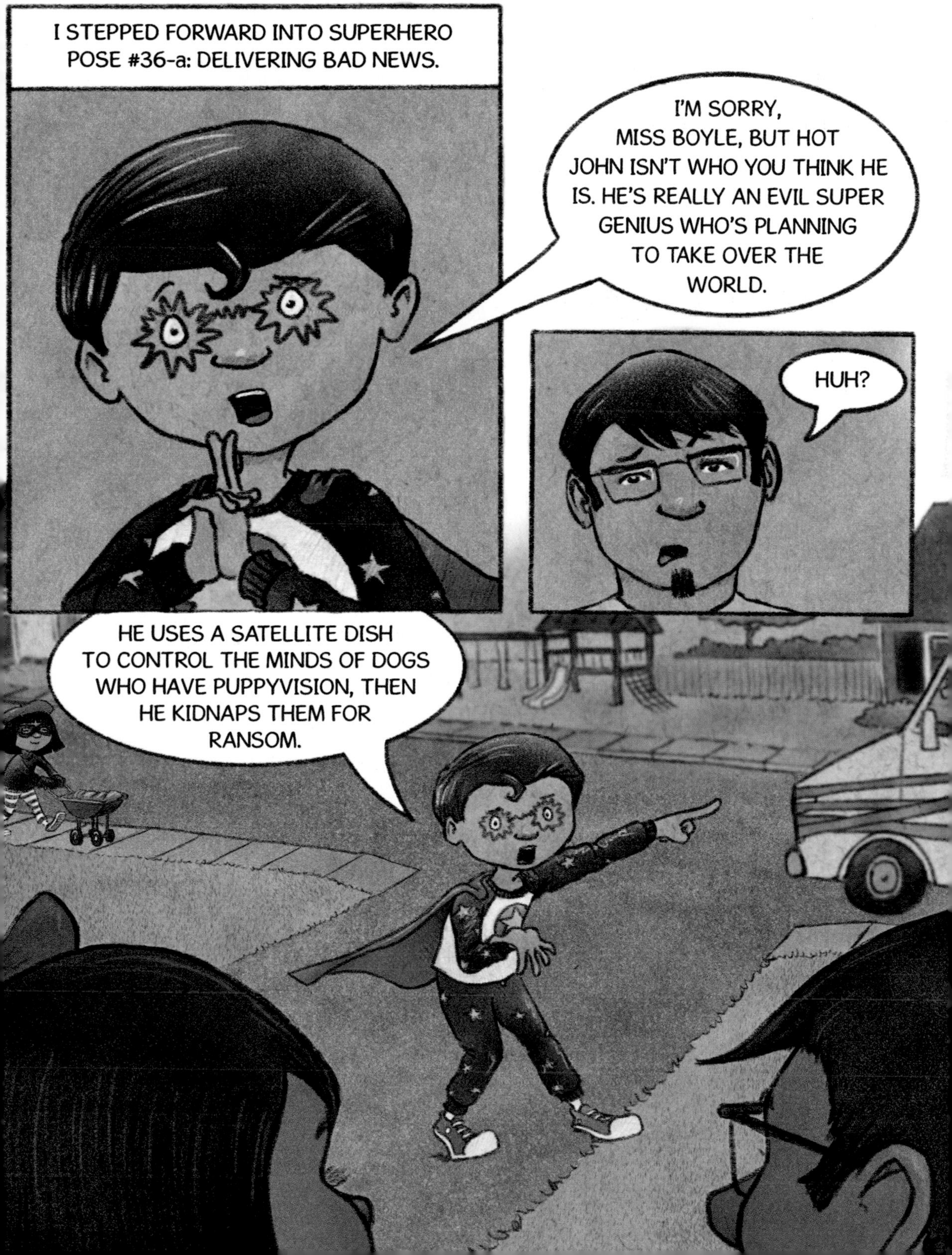
I STEPPED FORWARD INTO SUPERHERO POSE #36-a: DELIVERING BAD NEWS.
I'M SORRY, MISS BOYLE, BUT HOT JOHN ISN'T WHO YOU THINK HE IS. HE'S REALLY AN EVIL SUPER GENIUS WHO'S PLANNING TO TAKE OVER THE WORLD.
HUH?
HE USES A SATELLITE DISH TO CONTROL THE MINDS OF DOGS WHO HAVE PUPPYVISION, THEN HE KIDNAPS THEM FOR RANSOM.

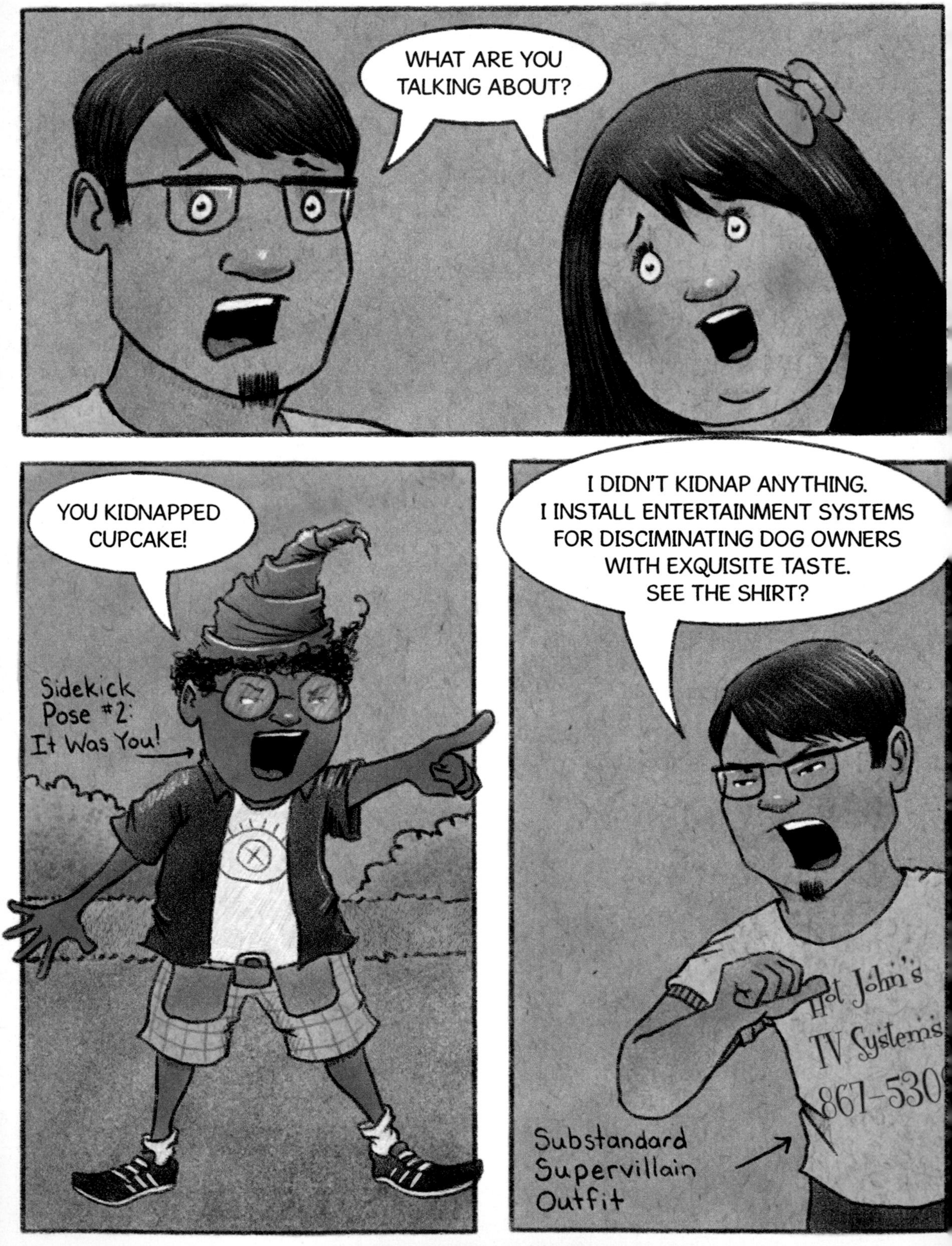
WHAT ARE YOU TALKING ABOUT?
YOU KIDNAPPED CUPCAKE!
Sidekick Pose #2: It Was You!
I DIDN'T KIDNAP ANYTHING. I INSTALL ENTERTAINMENT SYSTEMS FOR DISCIMINATING DOG OWNERS WITH EXQUISITE TASTE. SEE THE SHIRT?
Hot John's TV Systems
Substandard Supervillain Outfit

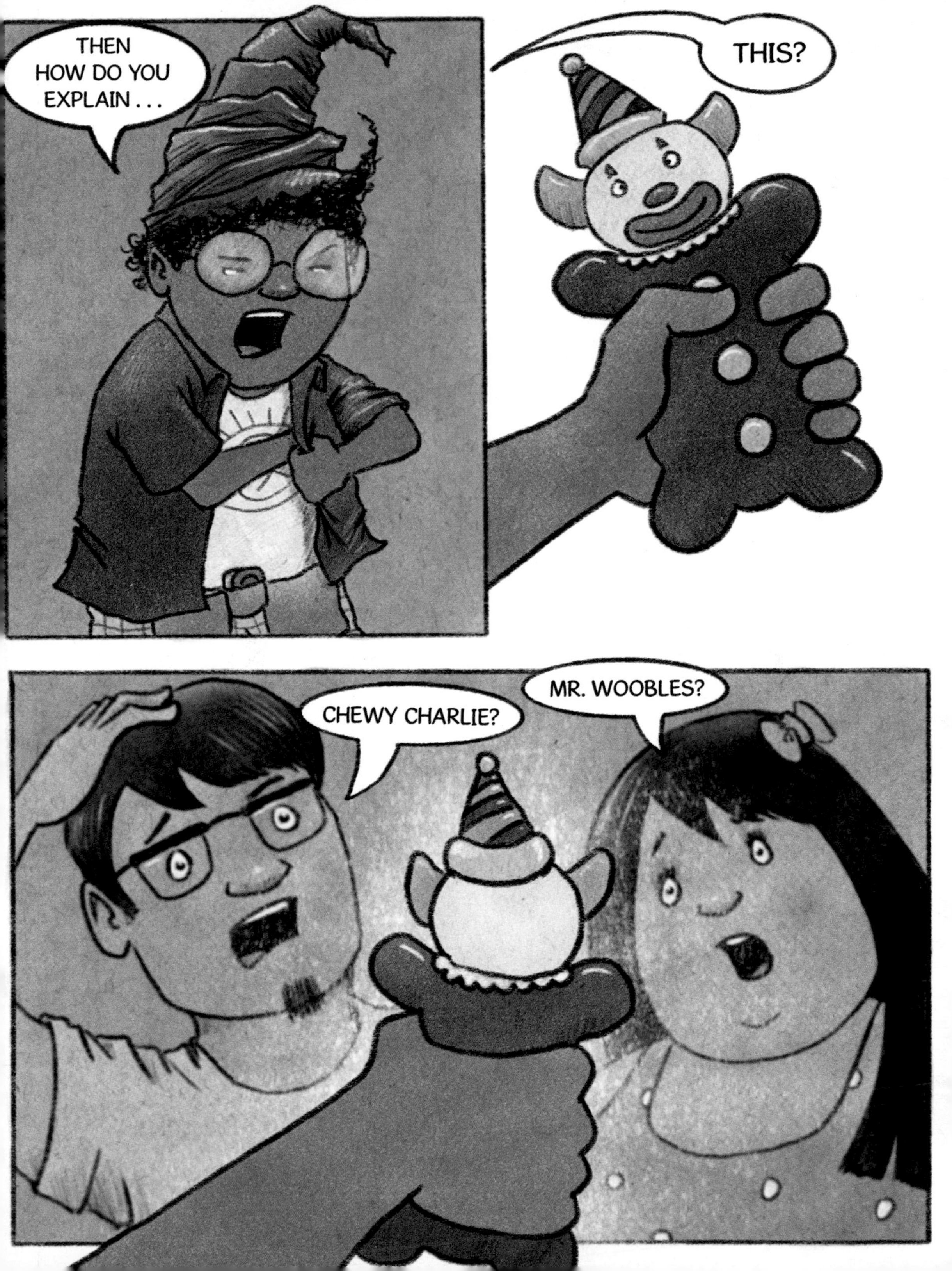
THEN HOW DO YOU EXPLAIN . . .
THIS?
CHEWY CHARLIE?
MR. WOOBLES?

"He's creating an army of Mr. Woobles clones to help him kidnap dogs," I announced.

"And this is the worst possible choice for a killer clone army, dude," Rudy said, shaking his head. "Seriously. A little squeaky toy? You should have picked something awesome to clone. Like a huge, fire-breathing hammerhead shark with laser-beam eyes and chainsaw teeth."

I marched up to Hot John. "If you didn't kidnap Cupcake, then why do you have Mr. Woobles?"

Rudy squeaked the Mr. Woobles clone a few times.

And that's when Cupcake came running into the driveway and jumped right into Miss Boyle's arms.

Chapter 16

SQUEALS OF JOY AND SQUEAKS OF CHEWY CHARLIE

Miss Boyle let out a squeal and snuggled into Cupcake's horrible, drooling, bug-eyed face. "Ooooohhhhh, Mama's wittul snoogy-poops is here, isn't she? Isn't she? Ooooohhhh, Mama was so worried about her wittul baby-puppy-Cuppy-Cuppy-Cupcake."

Abi followed Cupcake into the driveway. She was smiling a million megawatt smile.

Miss Boyle lifted her face out of Cupcake's belly and looked at us. "Now, will somebody PLEASE tell me what's going on here?"

"Yeah," Hot John said. "What's happening?"

"You should know, Hot John. You kidnapped Cupcake!" I cried. . . .

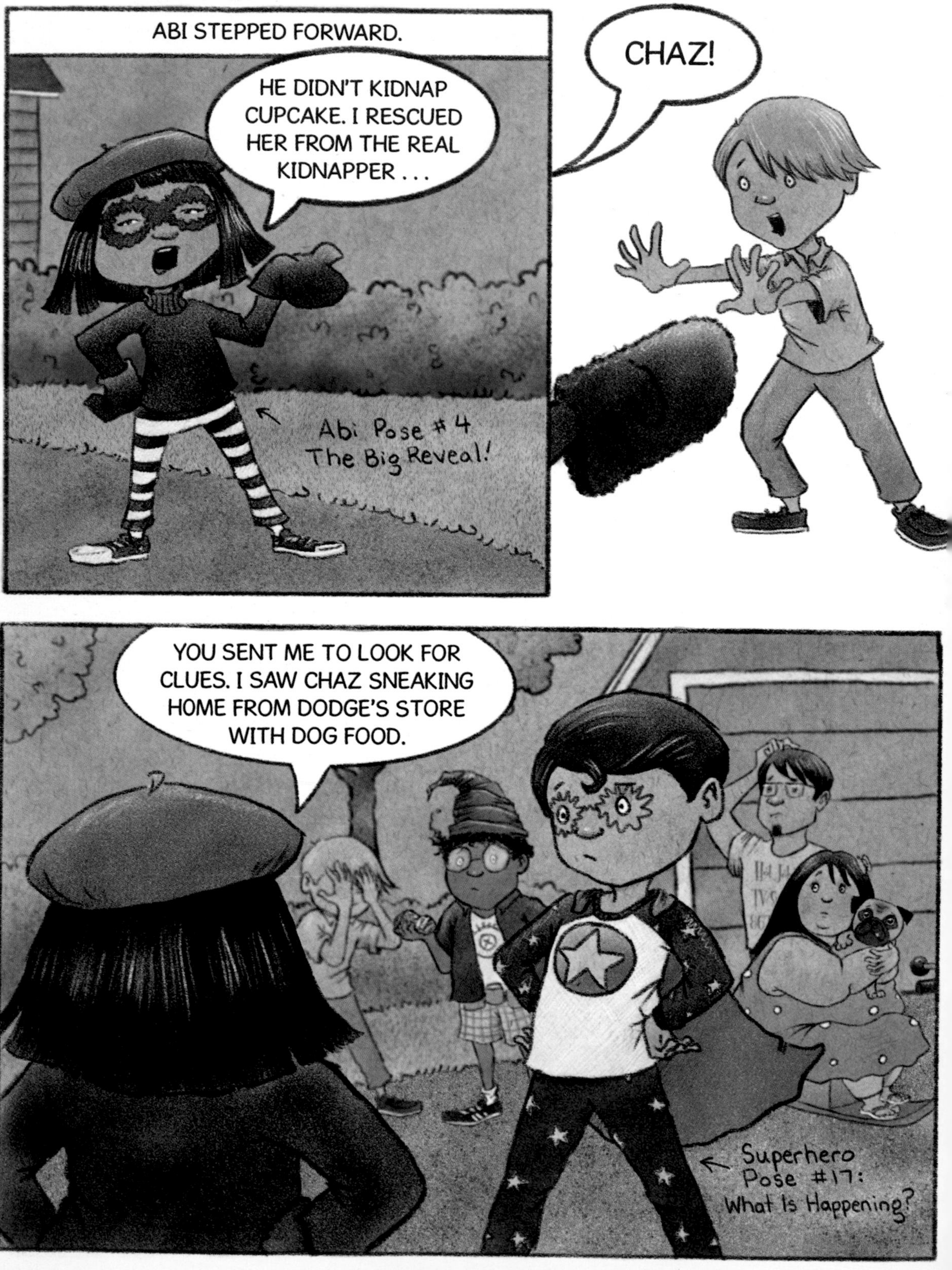
ABI STEPPED FORWARD.
HE DIDN'T KIDNAP CUPCAKE. I RESCUED HER FROM THE REAL KIDNAPPER . . .
Abi Pose #4 The Big Reveal!
CHAZ!
YOU SENT ME TO LOOK FOR CLUES. I SAW CHAZ SNEAKING HOME FROM DODGE'S STORE WITH DOG FOOD.
Superhero Pose #17: What Is Happening?

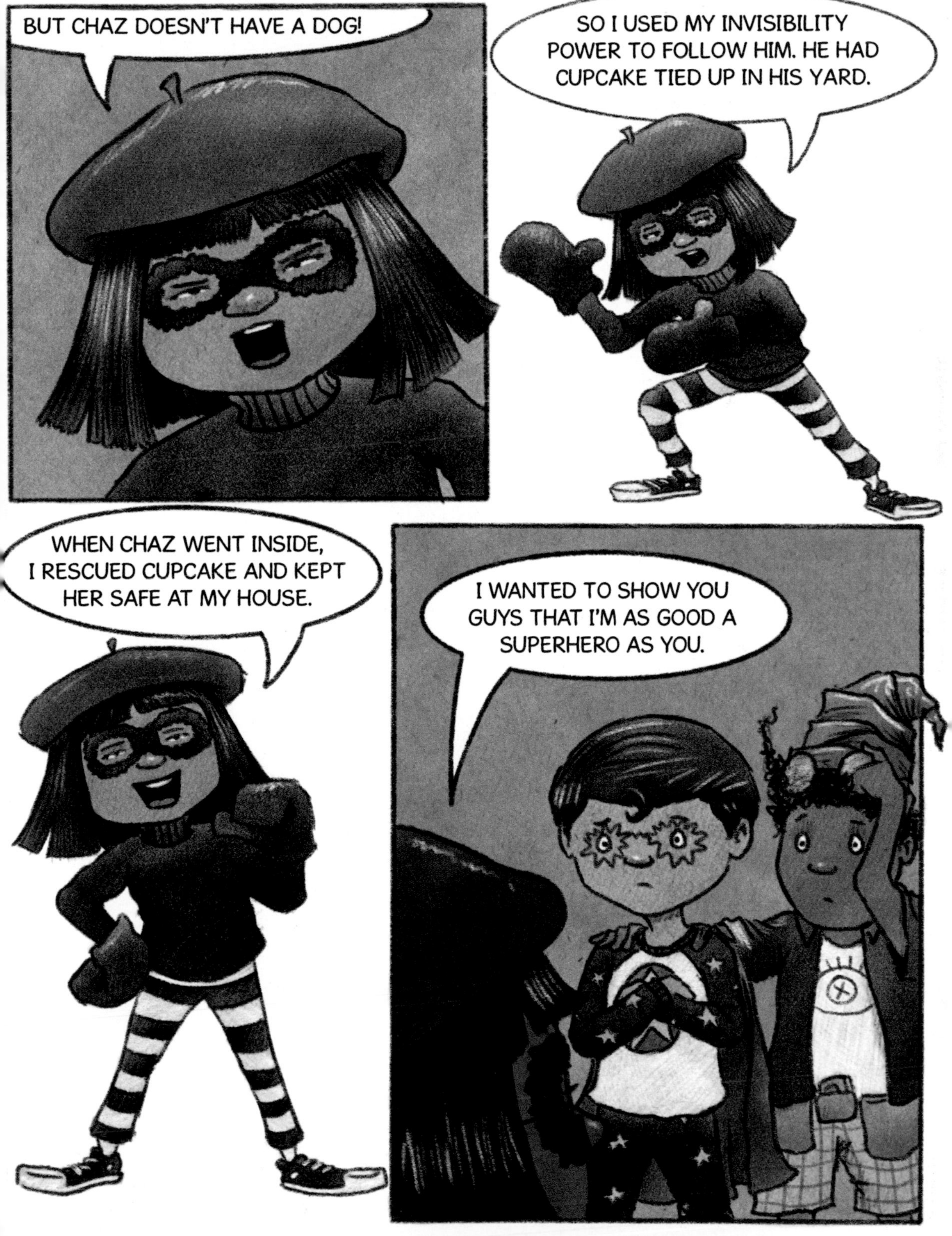
BUT CHAZ DOESN'T HAVE A DOG!
SO I USED MY INVISIBILITY POWER TO FOLLOW HIM. HE HAD CUPCAKE TIED UP IN HIS YARD.
WHEN CHAZ WENT INSIDE, I RESCUED CUPCAKE AND KEPT HER SAFE AT MY HOUSE.
I WANTED TO SHOW YOU GUYS THAT I'M AS GOOD A SUPERHERO AS YOU.

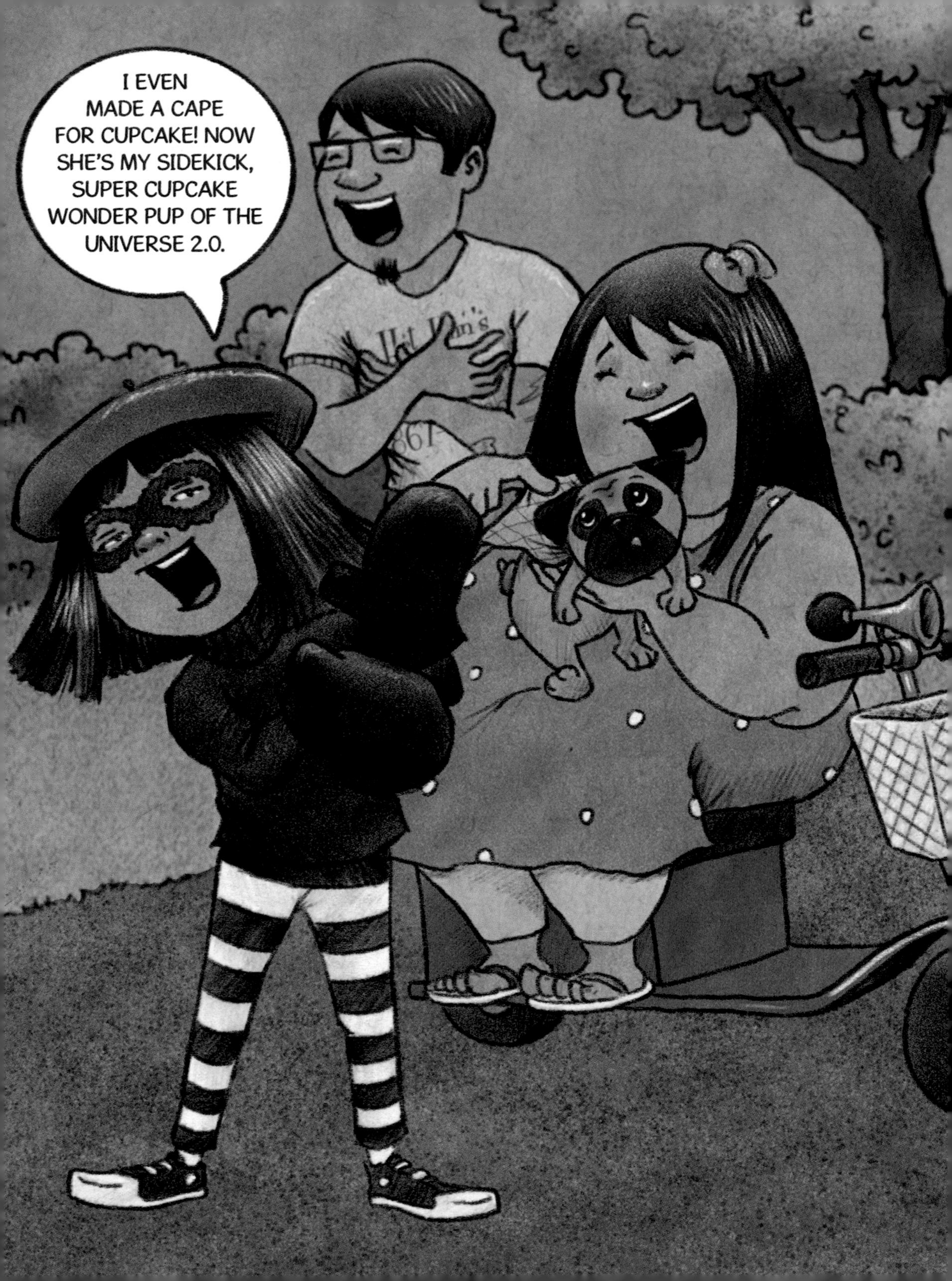
I EVEN MADE A CAPE FOR CUPCAKE! NOW SHE'S MY SIDEKICK, SUPER CUPCAKE WONDER PUP OF THE UNIVERSE 2.0.

This was not making perfect sense.

"But why was Mr. Woobles in Hot John's Evil Mobile?" I asked.

"It's not an Evil Mobile and that's not Mr. Woobles," Hot John snapped. "That's Chewie Charlie."

Hot John snatched Chewie Charlie from Rudy.

"I have Mr. Woobles," Abi said. She held up Cupcake's chew toy. She squeezed Mr. Woobles a few times. Cupcake howled with delight.

"He's Super Cupcake Wonder Pup of the Universe 2.0's sidekick. We call him Wonder Woobles Awesome Squeaky McGee."

"Whoa," Rudy whispered. "Even her sidekick has a sidekick. That's really cool."

"But why do you have an evil Mr. Woobles clone in your van?" I asked Hot John.

Hot John sighed and rolled his eyes. "It's not an evil clone. My own pug liked this toy so much, I had some made for advertising." He held it out so I could read the words "Hot John's TV Systems" printed on it. "I always keep a few of them in my van to give to customers."

He squeezed the chew toy. Cupcake barked and howled and panted with drooly delight. "Yeah? You like Chewie Charlie, too, Cupcake?" said Hot John. "Huh? Huh? Huh?"

"Awwwww," Miss Boyle said, "You have a wittul puppy-wuppy pug dog, too? What's his name?"

Hot John blushed and smiled. "Sprinkles."

"Sprinkles?" squealed Miss Boyle, "Oh my goodness, that is the most precious name. We should get our little babies together for a puggy play date. Cupcake and Sprinkles. Could anything be cuter?" She snuggled her face into Cupcake's belly again. "Does mummy's wittul Cupcake want a playdate with a new wittul fwiend? Huh? Does she? Does she? Does she?"

"But . . . but . . . but . . ." I stammered, pointing to Hot John. "What about the mind-control satellite dish on your van?"

"It's for advertising, too. I install satellite dishes, so I have a satellite dish on my van. Get it? It isn't even a real one. It's plastic. I got it at a yard sale for a buck."

"He buys his evil devices at yard sales?" Rudy sighed. "He's the absolute worst supervillain ever."

"But . . . but . . . what about the mutant, genetically modified squirrels?" I asked.

Hot John rolled his eyes. "I have no idea what you're talking about."

My shoulders dropped into a **NON-SUPERHERO POSE: DEFEATED**.

"I'm really sorry about Cupcake, Miss Boyle," I said. "I was trying so hard to be an awesome superhero."

"Well, I'm not happy that you weren't watching her at all times, Stevie," Miss Boyle said. "I thought you would be much more responsible. And Chaz, I'm extremely disappointed in you. I'm going to be talking to your parents about what you did. You should be ashamed of yourself. Cupcake will probably require months of intense therapy. She's very sensitive."

The Parasite nodded glumly as tears streaked down his cheeks.

"I'm really sorry, Miss Boyle," The Parasite sniffed. "I didn't want anything bad to happen to Cupcake. I just didn't want Stevie to get the money from you and buy the *Captain Fantastic* comic."

"Oh, Stevie won't be getting that money. He didn't watch my precious little Cupcake carefully. I'll be giving that money to Abi for taking such good care of Cupcake and saving the day."

She handed Abi a fat wad of cash and thanked her.

"What!?" I cried.

"Thank you, Miss Boyle," Abi said.

"And my name is Indestructible Abi Hammerfist of Lightning Adorability."

"That is SO cool," cried Rudy. "Why can't we think up awesome names like that?"

"I'm very disappointed in you boys," Miss Boyle said with a sigh. She smiled at Hot John. "But it looks like we have a happy ending, after all. Cupcake is home, safe and sound, and it looks like she's going to have a new friend. I'm having a birthday party for my little fuzzy bunkie-boo tonight. Would you like to come?"

Hot John gave Chewie Charlie a few squeaks.

Miss Boyle gave Mr. Woobles a few squeaks.

Both of them giggled.

Hot John turned to The Parasite and Rudy. "Why don't you guys take your buddy home, wash his face, and make him put on some clothes. Maybe do something about that hair?"

Rudy put his hand on my shoulder. "Let's go, dude."

The Parasite, Rudy, and I trudged down the sidewalk into the setting sun. Abi skipped along behind us, singing about the money Miss Boyle had given her.

Chapter 17

YET ANOTHER NEW ARCH-ENEMY

"I can't believe that Abi had Cupcake the entire time," The Parasite whined. "I'm in *so* much trouble."

"I can't believe I disappointed Miss Boyle like that," I groaned.

"Look on the bright side," Rudy said. "We still have awesome superpowers. We're still The Super Guys. Well, not you, Chaz. You stole Cupcake."

"Ha! You think I'd want to hang out with a bunch of super geeks like you?" The Parasite snarled. "It's your fault that I'm in such big trouble. You and your non-existent powers. And now I'm going to buy the *Captain Fantastic* comic on Monday morning. So long, losers."

"Good-bye, Parasite!" Abi sang, as he stormed off toward his lair. "Now that we got rid of him, we can go fight crime!"

"Abi," I sighed, "you're not a Super Guy. You hid Cupcake from us and got us in big trouble with Miss Boyle."

"I only did that to prove that I could be a Super Guy. I rescued Cupcake from The Parasite all by myself."

"Even if I wanted you to be a Super Guy—which I don't—you don't have any superpowers like we do," I told her.

"Yeah huhn I do," she said. "Remember? I can turn invisible. And I have a sidekick who has her own sidekick. Plus, I have my Super-Strength Heat-Proof Gloves of Awesomeness."

She held up her hands and shook the oven mitts at us.

"I don't care," I sighed. "It doesn't matter if we have superpowers or not. I disappointed an innocent citizen. I didn't act like a superhero. And if I don't get that copy of Captain Fantastic's secret training journal, I'll never learn how to be a superhero and control my awesome powers."

Abi waved the stack of bills in the air. "Yeah. I was thinking that I might buy that comic book for myself."

My heart sank. "What?!"

"If I was a Super Guy, I might let you read it."

"You would?" I asked. "Really, Super Abi?"

"Maybe," she said. "But now my name is Amazing Flash Quick-Draw Thunderpants the First!"

"Whoa . . ." gasped Rudy. "Awesome."

"Maybe after we get that top-secret journal, we can figure out who was controlling all those mutant squirrels," I said.

"Not again with the squir—" Rudy stopped walking and pointed at The Grassmaster's house. . . .

HE WAS SURROUNDED BY SQUIRRELS.

THE GRASSMASTER IS CONTROLLING THE . . .

SQUIRRELS!

I THINK WE'VE FOUND OUR NEW ARCH-ENEMY.

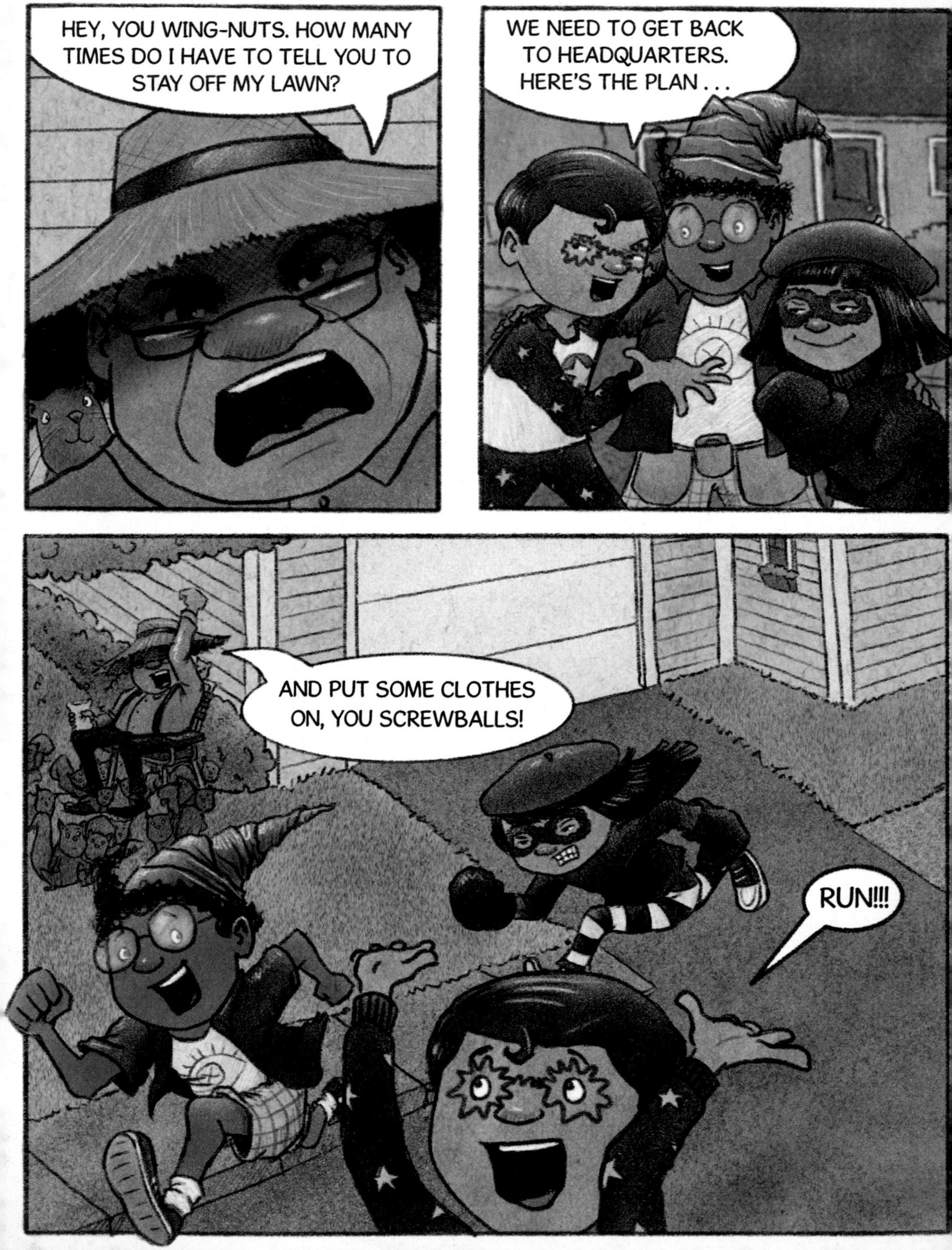
HEY, YOU WING-NUTS. HOW MANY TIMES DO I HAVE TO TELL YOU TO STAY OFF MY LAWN?
WE NEED TO GET BACK TO HEADQUARTERS. HERE'S THE PLAN . . .
AND PUT SOME CLOTHES ON, YOU SCREWBALLS!
RUN!!!

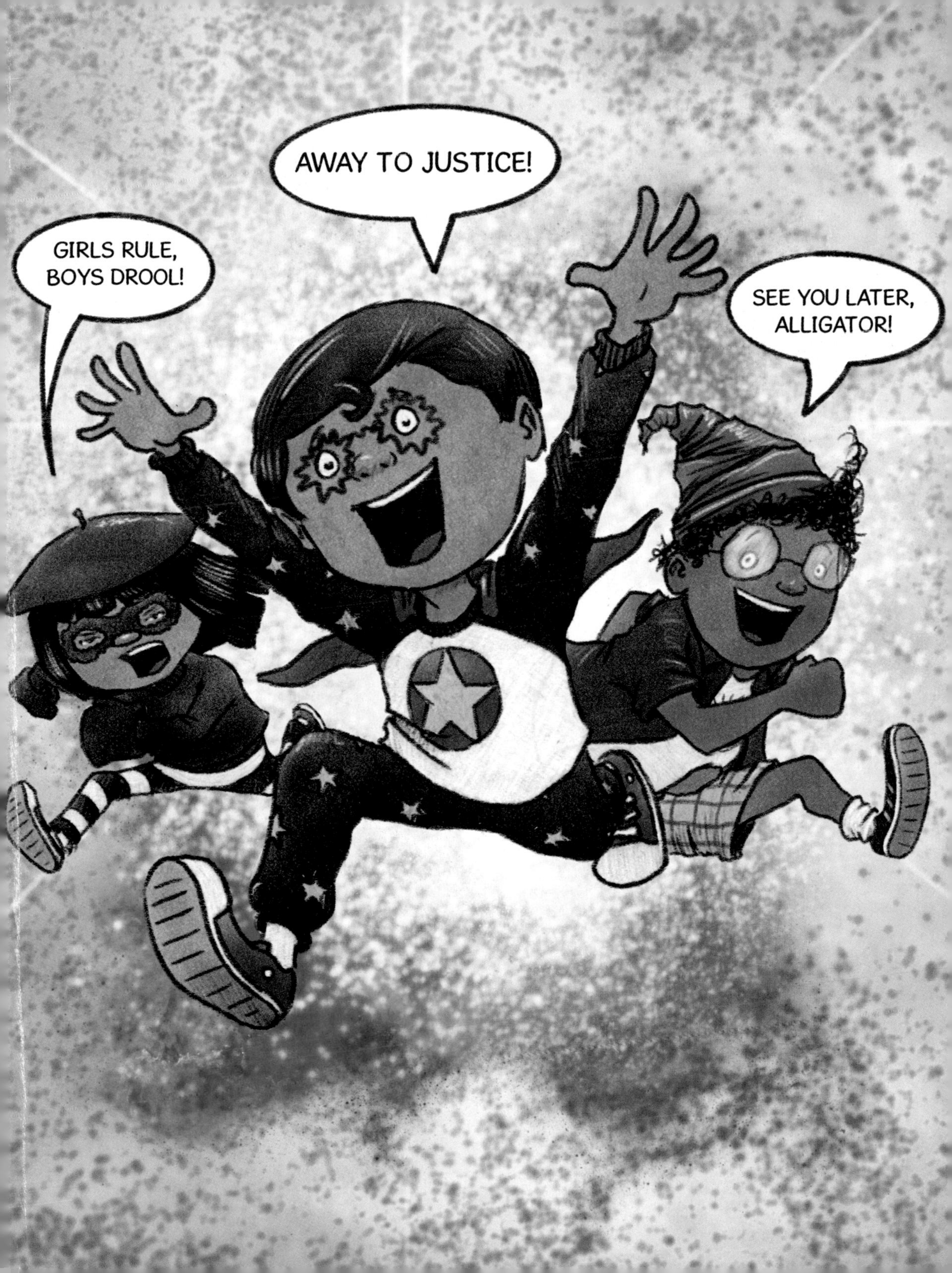
GIRLS RULE, BOYS DROOL!
AWAY TO JUSTICE!
SEE YOU LATER, ALLIGATOR!

ABOUT THE AUTHOR

MARTY KELLEY creates books, art, music, and tasty pizza from his top-secret headquarters deep in the woods of New Hampshire. His superpowers include: Funk-O-Matic Drumming Power; PizzaVision 2.0; Hyper-Honk Harmonica Skills; and Ultra-Mega-Deluxe Drawing Abilities. Marty loves visiting schools, walking alone through the woods, and listening to podcasts. But not all at the same time. Find out more at his website: www.martykelley.com.